Treble Clef

Malcolm Hollingdrake

Book Eight in the Harrogate Crime Series

ISBN: 978-1-9160715-7-5

Praise for Malcolm Hollingdrake

This is a gripping tale which is written well and paced perfectly. I was pretty engrossed rather quickly and particularly appreciated the discussion of scientific stuff which certainly sets this book apart from the rest of the crime genre. The only other books I know that do this is the amazing CSI Eddie Collins series by Andrew Barrett. The perspectives were also pretty interesting, especially the point-of-view of the unidentified killer, I can't remember the last time I read a crime novel that includes the killer's POV but it works incredibly well and kept the story fresh and interesting. The other POV is that of DCI Bennett, which talks about his father's death as well as the case. I must admit that I loved the effortlessness of the prose as it made the story very readable with everything flowing beautifully chapter-to-chapter, and I had quite a bit of trouble putting it down due to this.

Lou – Top 500 Amazon Reviewer.

To me crime books need that background of characters so that they are not "just about the job" and Malcolm always does this so very well. Cyril and his team come alive on the pages and the snaps of background give them that reality factor.
Another brilliant read from Cyril and Malcolm, I very much look forward to the next one.

Misfits farm – Book reviews

The research by the author is just outstanding again, he is a perfectionist with his story lines and very unusual methods of killing. Extremely original and totally gripping, these books are classy with humour in perfect balance!

Susan Hampson – Books from Dusk Till Dawn – Book Blogs.

A great book with Malcolm's now trademark mix of technical research and knowledge, character build, use of God's own country for a backdrop and a plot that keeps you hooked until that moment where you realise you missed it too... not just Cyril.

Leeds Buyer – Amazon Review

Also by

Malcolm Hollingdrake

Bridging the Gulf

Shadows from the Past
Short Stories for Short Journeys

The Harrogate Crime Series

Only the Dead

Hell's Gate

Flesh Evidence

Game Point

Dying Art

Crossed Out

The Third Breath

Treble Clef

Dedicated to

Ruth, Ann and John Eagin.

Remembering

A. E. Eagin MM

1918

In the animal kingdom, one of the keys to survival is to outwit your enemies.

Neil deGrasse Tyson

Prologue

"Trompe l'oeil." The words sounded on the lips like a forbidden fruit as they were repeated a number of times. On each occasion different elements were exaggerated. "It has a certain ring to it, a... je ne sais quoi... a kind of magic mixed with a hint of mystery that allows the eye to confuse the brain. The two-dimensional wall becomes three-dimensional or that is the appearance it gives and that is the whole point... to create something that does not really exist. It only seems to appear in the eyes of the beholder. It will help them suspend their disbelief and that is all it takes... Trompe l'oeil."

The large bristles of the paintbrush continued to apply the light stippling. Finer brushes bled in the detail and on standing back, the wall had the appearance of a police cell dating back to the sixties. The lights were turned down and the atmosphere changed significantly.

"It's so simple to create. Without smoke and mirrors the place simply changes and with their help..."

The paints and trays were collected and the light extinguished. It was nearly ready.

Chapter One

The charity shop, situated on Harrogate's Montpellier Hill, appearing squashed between a bar and an art gallery, had seen a steady stream of customers for a midweek day – especially considering the capricious nature of the weather. The grey cloud mantle showed clear signs of receding as the day lengthened, leaving only the occasional brisk but often short shower. The majority of customers had been visitors to Harrogate, according to Valerie Thew, who had worked in the shop voluntarily for the past four years; she had a nose for these things. Guessing their status in life and their hometown had been a game she had developed and would often play to alleviate the tedium on quiet days. It was a personal challenge but recently, on occasion, she had started to share her perceptions with her colleagues; *the Svengali gift,* as she had incorrectly called it. She had the impression that a Svengali could see the impossible and Valerie had no idea or desire to know the truth. In her mind a Svengali was someone who had a controlling and possibly sinister influence over others, but then no one corrected her because maybe they believed the metaphorical hat might just about fit.

Valerie could not recall when the habit of people watching had started, nor could she remember the first time she had made judgements on their circumstances and character; somehow it had always seemed so obvious, to be part of her make-up, her very DNA; a gift she had often boasted of. Was it when she was at school? She could not recollect. What she did know was that it happened almost daily, briefly it must be said, but daily and it amused her.

On summer days when time hung loosely like a luffing sail she would sit and watch people. She had become fascinated by their mannerisms and what she interpreted to be idiosyncrasies; how she loved that word. She had a particular

1

fondness for both the particularly young and the old. To her, however, the young were those older than twenty. These judgements would fuel her imagination and very soon a whole fictitious scenario would be played out in her mind with the innocent street *actors* being totally unaware of her personal, imaginary theatre. She would give them names, accents and social class, stammers and impediments, even emotional baggage to enhance the mind games she played. Only she heard their conversations, felt their happiness and their anguish, but then, only she cared. This belief that she was blessed with a strange power was not a snobbish affectation. She truly believed she had a gift and she could see what those around could not.

The elderly lady had been in the shop for a few minutes before allowing her fingers to run along the length of the clothes hanging on the rail like a pianist silently caressing the keys. Stopping occasionally, she extracted various sleeves, holding them against the skin of her hand before tucking them back with little regard. It was a sudden and almost brutal action that saw her extract from the collection a bright yellow blouse. Dropping her bag securely by her feet, she held the garment against her and turned to look in the mirror. The sequence of actions made Valerie grimace. That frown concealed the intrigue she felt growing. A false image came to her mind's eye with great clarity, a mirage, hazy at first but slowly growing more clear by the second.

She pictured the woman standing in front of a small cooker in a one bedroom flat, possibly in Bradford, maybe Shipley. A cigarette was hanging from the side of her mouth. Ash fell casually like dandruff, contrasting sharply with the wisp of smoke travelling heavenward. *To heaven and to hell,* she said quietly to herself. The smell of stale fat and fags hung heavily in the imaginary air. Valerie could make out the curlers wrapped tightly in her hair and partly enclosed in a flower-patterned scarf to complete the mental vignette. She would know more of that place when the woman spoke. Valerie seemed to be able to glean most from her auditory sense but what she did know was the woman was out for the day and hoping to find a bargain; after all, the inhabitants of the North Yorkshire town were considered affluent and there were likely to be better pickings from their donated items than those in the shops situated in the big cities.

"That looks very nice, the warm colour would brighten any day. It suits your complexion." Valerie's voice seemed outwardly sincere and brought a smile to the stranger's lips. "The lemon yellow brings colour to your complexion... It's very flattering... As I said, it suits you."

"Do you think so? I wasn't too sure." She looked across at Valerie hoping for a second helping of complimentary words. Her speech clearly changed from her normal to a more pretentious enunciation in an attempt to convey a different social standing. Her words were a little too exaggerated and Valerie knew the diction was false.

Valerie looked away momentarily but still watched the customer surreptitiously check the price tag before looking in the mirror a second time. Turning back Valerie nodded again. "Suits you, really."

"It's a great style, and was once expensive I bet you." The flat vowel burst from the word, *great*, like truth carelessly flushed from a vocal lie and exposing the customer's attempt at appearing refined.

Bradford, Valerie said to herself and that brought an even greater feeling of satisfaction; she was getting so accurate but she still needed the confirmation. "Did you come on the bus today?"

The shopper collected her bag before handing the blouse to Valerie.

"No, my son is working here for the day and he brought me in his..." she paused before continuing, as if she were embarrassed... "Car. It's a new one too. He spoils me."

"Travelled far?" Valerie placed the blouse in a recycled plastic bag and handed her the change.

"No, Bradford, forty minutes, that's all. Nice to get out into the fresh air." The word sounded like *Bratford*.

Valerie could not help but repeat the word *Bradford* in a surprised tone but she felt triumphant inside. She had considered whether to mimic the word emphasising the mysterious letter *t* but decided against it.

"I only popped in to pick up a cheap brolly, left mine in the va… car." She quickly corrected her error, but her face still flushed red.

"Sold the last one about an hour ago, sorry. We've had a run on umbrellas but then that's normal when the weather proves so unpredictable. We can never get enough."

As the customer put her change away, Valerie moved towards the door. She pulled it open, the action bringing with it the familiar chime from the small bell. "Thank you for popping in. Enjoy the rest of your stay in Harrogate and have a safe run home in the va…" she paused wanting to say *van*, cruelly, but stopped herself. She did, however, allow her accent to mimic that of the customer's fake snobbish tone. It was clearly part of the game she played. The now embarrassed customer flushed red again. "…car journey home."

Valerie watched her turn quickly and scurry up Montpellier Hill before moving back into the shop. She chuckled to herself but stopped momentarily as she realised that those brief moments outside in the fresh air had suddenly resurrected the shop's familiar smell to invade her nostrils. It was never pleasant but she knew it could soon be banished. Over the course of the day she had grown accustomed to the compensatory, masking smell that artificially drowned the stale aroma that permeated from tightly railed, second-hand clothes. *The stink,* as Valerie referred to it could be temporarily banished with an air freshener. Leaning under the counter she collected the aerosol and sprayed the shop before checking her watch.

***

At the flick of the remote, the garage door juddered momentarily before beginning to rise noiselessly. It was

4

allowed to progress until it was a third of the way up. Kevin Carruthers's finger swiftly activated the *stop* button. It was enough for the average height adult to slip below and in. Kevin bent and moved forward as if to limbo dance under the door. The courtesy light had already illuminated automatically and would remain on for three minutes after the door had rolled down to the closed position; before then, the main lights had been switched on.

The internal space had been sectioned. The first quarter of the room looked like any other of the garages in the row, the exposed brick and unpainted concrete floor seemed positively austere. Three bicycles hung from metal, purpose-made brackets, screwed to the wooden rafters by their front wheels as if convicted and condemned for capital misdemeanours. Picking up a cloth he wiped the frame of the nearest and his newest bike.

There was to the right a steel clothing rack on four small, wheeled feet. Hanging from this were cycling clothes, all bright Lycra, and below on the wooden shelf, four pairs of shoes that had the appearance of tight ankle boots. He took the recently washed clothing he had brought in and hung it on hangers before adding the clothes to the rack. Other small accoutrements linked with his cycling hobby were dotted on shelves. Three posters showing images of the *Tour de Yorkshire* were pinned to the rear stud wall next to which was a door. It was behind this that the ambience of this garage changed.

Here the walls were lined and painted a satin black. The floor was carpeted, again in a dark colour but now charcoal grey. However, it took on a darker appearance owing to the depth of colour reflected by the walls. Along the two sides were glass-fronted, illuminated cabinets containing hundreds of small figures, each beautifully painted. To discern their features and the quality of the paintwork they would have to be studied in daylight but they were all subtly different. A table sat squarely in the centre of the room and four high back chairs were positioned at each face, the seats, tucked under, concealed below the table top. A pendulum light hung a metre above, the metal shade also black.

The most bizarre element of the whole space sat on the shelves above the cabinets and if counted, the observer would note they totalled twenty-two.

On the very far wall were shelves containing boxes of games, all orderly and immaculately presented. It was clear to any casual observer this sanctum was, to the owner at least, a very special space and one that was treated with utmost reverence. Kevin opened the second cabinet and removed a solitary figure; it was neither human nor animal. Bizarrely, he brought it to his lips and kissed it. *We shall work together, and we shall be the victors*, he said to himself as he tucked the figure into a small soft cloth bag before turning to the miniature security camera positioned to the left of the penultimate object along the shelf. Connected to the mains it would record, should sound or movement trigger a response. Images would then be stored on the loop of the mini disc. Normally this would give an hour's viewing of the captured moments. In most cases there was nothing; the banging from another garage or even a wagon passing the road had triggered the camera. He had planned to install a device that would send the images to his phone on activation but the cost had proved prohibitive, besides he had no Wi-Fi connection in the garage.

Closing the inner door, he moved past the cycles. "Open!" his whispered command made him smile as his finger touched the remote. He watched the door rise again and left, pausing until it had closed fully.

***

Within half an hour the shop would close and Valerie could walk back to her apartment, slip off her shoes, feed Monty the cat and have a cup of tea before getting ready. She smiled to herself as thoughts of her evening, that she had managed to keep secret, brought a flutter to her stomach. It was the first time for many months she was going on a date. Or was it a year? She checked her calendar and was surprised to see it had been thirteen months! How time was flying by. It would be nothing fancy, a stroll along The Stray if the weather continued to improve and a drink in possibly *The Old Swan Hotel* or *The George*. She was filled with an almost forgotten excitement and if she were honest, a frisson of anxiety as well; either way it was euphoric.

The sound of the doorbell broke her thoughts and two more customers walked into the shop. She smiled politely.

Valerie's world had been exposed to new opportunities since her friend had persuaded her to join the local U3A. She had chuckled at the thought of being in The University of the Third Age. She reminded herself that apart from her Svengali gift, she had neither been clever nor motivated enough to attend a university of the first age when she was younger, let alone now when there were times she could not remember what day it was, or when she found herself standing between rooms wondering why she was there. She held that thought in her head as she bagged the items of clothing and a pair of shoes one of the customers had placed on the counter. She was going through the motions but maintained a smile, ignoring the belief that bad luck might come to those who carelessly place footwear where they had. As the customers left, the familiar tinkle of the bell seemed louder somehow as the door opened and closed, leaving the shop empty apart from its familiar aroma and the late sun's dappled rays dancing on the empty counter. To Valerie the jittering was not unlike the butterflies that had returned to her stomach but, as it was time to close, they were even stronger than before.

Chapter Two

The players, the majority of whom were leaning away from the game table, were deep in concentration. The ambient yellow light brought a silent yet competitive air to the room. The atmosphere had changed and seemed to hang heavily like smoke as the night progressed. For one player, the game was his, the *Secret* card he had been dealt was clearly marked *Betrayer*. The others would have realised had he not possessed the skill to mask his advantage with nonchalance. As a seasoned player he knew just how to conceal his growing hold over the game. He still held his cards cautiously, maintaining a façade that concealed his strategy. Overconfidence, the wrong facial expression, a simple gesture when decisions had to be taken collectively, or wrong posture could bring about a sudden disadvantage. It was about distraction without overcompensation and the ability to watch and observe mistakes in others before taking the initiative and acting swiftly and decisively at the right moment, a time of weakness; it had to be remembered that they, the group, had many chances, he had but one. He was, however, rewarded by seeing the group's *morale score* slowly falling towards the target marked on his *Secret* card and should it reach that then the game was his.

The other players were working to determine a positive outcome, to keep the zombies at bay, and so far they had co-operated well and identified whom they believed to be the traitor in the group, soon putting paid to that player's continued involvement. The exposed traitor now sat and reflected on his denouement. It had not been a classic game and his card draw had conspired against his plan, certainly with results he had not anticipated and therefore clearly had not expected. He had allowed himself to be exposed and he replayed the error over in his head a number of times. However, the second traitor had covered his path so well and Kevin had taken the game.

"One final drink and a new game tomorrow?" They laughed as they congratulated Kevin. "Bloody dark horse you. Working with the dead all day that does it. Help from the underworld no doubt."

Life did not get much better as Kevin's hand, deep in his pocket, caressed the concealed figure wrapped in the soft cloth bag, his lucky amulet. This sudden enthusiasm and the word *dead* were the catalysts that made his excited mind rewind and replay. He suddenly visualised the corpse he had been dealing with seventy-two hours previously. In the early hours a young life had been taken in an adrenalin-rushed manoeuvre during a high-powered motorcycle dash through the narrow country lanes of North Yorkshire. He remembered the very morning. It had been the start of what was to be a beautiful day, the dawn's coloured palette bringing myriad shades of orange and yellow to the landscape.

The biker had not been totally oblivious as to what might be round the next corner and he had scanned the road ahead for potential hazards. At that moment, the sound of his bike and its sheer power pumped vitality through his body. He had smiled momentarily. Life was good. The body of the badger, struck earlier by a motorist, had lain tucked on the very edge of the bend just where the road surface joined the grass verge, its back broken when it had impacted with the car. Its front legs still twitched but were useless. This prone and partially concealed creature would be enough to catapult the rider and the bike over the hedge and towards the unforgiving oak tree. The damage to the rider's face had been considerable as the helmet had taken the initial impact, but in doing so it had split and flown off. The pursuing, tumbling machine, his pride and joy moments before, had glanced off the tree and conspired against him. The splintered front forks of the motorcycle had found his face ensuring his life, now on the very edge, was immediately extinguished. His crumpled body and bike had remained there for a number of hours, only being discovered by chance.

Kevin had prepared bodies for viewing on many occasions, some unfortunately with disfigured features, but this case proved to be very demanding. Maybe it was because the death had come on two wheels and he knew himself from some of the close calls he had experienced that death could be a moment away. The picture he now visualised in his mind's eye was as clear as if the body were laid out before him. He shuddered.

"Cheers and congratulations, Kevin!" A number of hands patted his shoulders as they drank the final victor's toast. "Until tomorrow when we seek our revenge."

Kevin closed his eyes as if to wash the image from his thoughts. He smiled and downed the drink. The route back to his accommodation would, he hoped, be a time to clear his head but he seemed to be slowly growing more and more disorientated. He had remembered a route that seemed familiar, but became confused and he stopped at the junction of Strawberry Dale Avenue and Franklin Road just to get his bearings. He wished now he had gone straight home from the Convention Centre as that would have made life easier. The incline in the road to his left reassured him that he must turn and go that way. The route seemed quiet and the streetlight shone through the occasional roadside trees casting dappled, soft-moving shadows across the dark paving. It was almost kaleidoscopic and discomfiting. The slight movement brought immediate uncertainty, dislocation and a strong feeling of nausea. He paused whilst leaning on a stone wall trying to concentrate on the road ahead and to regain his composure as well as his sense of direction.

"Are you alright?"

Kevin tried to focus on the face of the person who stood some distance away.

"Are you looking for anywhere in particular?" The voice was steady, confident and reassuring.

"*The Grey House*. I feel like death... I'm staying at *The Grey House*. I thought it was this way but... and I've drunk very lit..." He did not finish his sentence and his voice seemed shaky and distant.

"Don't worry, I can help." A hand took his elbow. "You're closer than you think. Not far. I'll look on it as my good deed for the day, my random act of kindness."

Kevin was immediately taken by the smell, a sweet attractive scent that flooded his nostrils; it seemed familiar. The firm grip that now supported his arm and helped to steady him took control. Nothing else was said but Kevin could hear his own breathing which seemed laboured as they progressed up the hill.

Within minutes Kevin could see the familiar front door and thanked his *shepherd* who had seemingly vanished once he had been ushered through the gate. Even in his confused state, this act brought to his mind the short story written by Frederick Forsyth in which a plane had guided another aircraft lost in the cloud... "*The Shepherd*, yes that was the title," he mumbled to himself whilst fumbling for his keys. Turning he whispered, "Thank you, *shepherd*. Let's hope you weren't a ghost."

Had he taken a moment to focus, had he the ability to look into the shadows beyond the gate, he would have seen the hand rise in response.

Despite being faced with three different shaped keys on the one ring he soon managed to open the front door and then the vestibule. There was a slight smell of cooked food but instead of being an unpleasant aroma, he suddenly felt hungry. He stood momentarily and gave himself a firm talking to. *You're working too hard, you need some time off, recharge the batteries. What with the new flat, this convention and rebuilding the faces of the foolish.* He took a run at the stairs grasping hold of the handrail. Soon he was in his room. He drank some water and felt refreshed. The bed looked so inviting but he was determined to undress. Within five minutes his clothes were tidied and his head hit the pillow. He neither heard the front door open nor the ring of the vestibule bell and by the time his bedroom door opened he was fast asleep.

Chapter Three

Cyril approached the *The Grey House* bed and breakfast accommodation leaving behind him a thin haze of white vapour. The officer manning the front garden gate had recognised his rank from the shine to his shoes and lifted the police tape in anticipation. He smiled. Cyril tucked away his e-cigarette and carefully walked on the protective step plates positioned in front of the house before mounting the three stone steps. He felt a little like Hansel following the bread trail and smiled before realising the reason he was there… The wicked witch in this case had long since fled, if it were indeed a she. These days you could never be sure.

On seeing Cyril approach, the Crime Scene Manager opened the vestibule door, the action ringing the small bell that was attached. Cyril studied the offending article. He sniffed and was sure he could smell vomit. He had always had a strange aversion to body fluids, particularly when they were not his. He checked the soles of his shoes just in case.

"That's the security system, sir." He smiled at Cyril.

"What is?"

"The bell, sir." He opened and closed the door again so that Cyril could hear it and raised his eyebrows before quickly continuing. "DS Owen is in the breakfast area, sir." He noted the time of Cyril's arrival and pointed to the room.

Owen was busy staring at an electronic tablet and in his peripheral vision noticed Cyril enter the room. Instinctively he immediately handed it over.

"Morning, sir. Not too pretty but I've seen worse."

Had it not been for the two vivid red areas contrasting with the white of the thin sheet covering the body, laid out in what was clearly a foetal position, DCI Cyril Bennett might have been forgiven for considering the person to be sleeping.

He stared at the image on the electronic tablet. Moving his fingers on the screen to enlarge and focus on the only visible part of skin that was showing proved difficult but with Owen's help he was soon rewarded. He stared at a hand that protruded from the sheet and overhung the side of the bed, palm uppermost, fingers together as if in supplication. The pale skin contrasted with the dark coloured carpet. He sucked in his lips and tilted his head to one side and then the other before slipping his glasses to the top of his head. He handed the tablet back to Owen.

"Well, Owen?"

"Kevin Carruthers. Checked in two days ago. Staying whilst attending a board gaming convention that's planned over four days. It's the small patch lower down the sheet that worries me."

Cyril continued to look at Owen, who had arrived at the crime scene fifteen minutes before him. Crease lines formed across Cyril's forehead that told Owen his boss was about to ask a question he probably would not have the answer to. "Christ, Owen, don't tell me he plays Cluedo?" The tone of Cyril's voice had a cynical rawness as he rolled his electronic cigarette across his lower lip and extended the first syllable in the word, *Cluedo*.

"Cluedo, sir?" Owen repeated with the same elongation. "I don't know…" He paused considering the question again but was still none the wiser. He shook his head.

"Never mind, Owen. Probably a tad before your time."

Owen shrugged before he continued to brief Cyril. "What I do know is he attended the convention. There the punters play games and manufacturers and traders sell all kinds of board games and other stuff. Hundreds attend. You've seen them in town, always have the lanyard and pass around their necks. That way they can identify each other no doubt, challenge each other to tiddly-winks and the like…" He looked at Cyril and smiled but there was little facial response.

Cyril quickly realised Owen had known all along.

"We understand he returned here just after eleven last night but failed to come down for breakfast. In fact, it was only when the cleaner went to make up his room that he was discovered."

"Mrs Peacock in the conservatory with a candlestick," Cyril mumbled to himself.

"Sir?" Owen watched Cyril stop and focus. "Mrs Peacock?"

"Sorry, lost for a minute in my past. And the cleaner's name?"

"Janet Johnson. She's in the kitchen with Simon. He's the owner. As you can imagine she's devastated. The reason for the vomit at the top of the steps apparently... well, as I said, she was shocked."

"Thought I got a whiff when I came in." Cyril checked his watch, shook his wrist and checked again. "What time did the convention close?"

Owen knew he could not plead ignorance. "We're looking into that now, sir." There was a long pause before Cyril spoke, making Owen shuffle uncomfortably.

"Take me through what we do know from the time he was discovered and take it step by step, up until the CSI people arrived."

Owen confidently checked through the notes he had made and took a deep breath as he scanned the page. "A 999 call came from the owner into control at 10.47. Reported finding..."

"And his name?"

"Sorry, yes, Simon, Simon Lee. As I said he reported finding Mr Carruthers's body. I said he's in the kitchen with..."

"The cleaner, yes, Owen, I recall."

Owen paused. It was going to be one of those days. "I listened to that call and Mr Lee appeared calm considering what he and his member of staff had just discovered." Owen paused and observed Cyril's expression before continuing. "Usual advice from Control regarding further entry to the room etc and to ensure everyone else present stays away as much as possible from the route into the house and the scene, but to remain on the premises. Paramedic arrived at the same time as the officers... 10.58. He checked the deceased and then gave the cleaner the once over."

"For what, Owen?"

"Checked her for signs of shock and advised she didn't need any further treatment but would receive police support." Owen shook his head convinced that Cyril knew what he meant in the first place. "They secured the site, made a list of the details of those present and those checked in. Police doctor arrived 11.15 closely followed by crime scene team. Doctor's up there now and also two CSI officers who kindly posted these early pictures." He flicked over the page to ensure he had not omitted anything and then wiped his mouth on the sleeve of his jacket.

Cyril looked round the breakfast room. The whiff of bacon still lingered alongside the smell of toast, a kinder aroma than the one with which he had been greeted. The white wooden shutters on the windows, although open, allowed only a limited view onto the garden to the front and to the side car park. The radio, positioned on the corner of the sideboard, was still on but the volume was set low. He let his eyes scan more of the room until they stopped at the two large ceramic cockerels placed on either end of the mantelpiece.

Owen had watched him take in the room. "You'll not find a better brace of cocks than them!" The tone of Owen's voice did not mask the innuendo.

Cyril said nothing and the pause was palpable.

Owen shuffled uncomfortably. "There are four guests waiting in the lounge, sir. I organised Smirthwaite to come down to take statements so we can get them out of the way. There are two other couples. One left early but will be returning later today and the other has checked out." He glanced at his notes but was interrupted as DC Brian Smirthwaite came into the room.

"Morning... God! What a great smell. I could kill for a bacon roll."

16

Owen looked at his watch. "Morning's nearly over, Brian... Just... You're late."

"Someone might have done just that, Brian," Cyril answered before noting his colleague's countenance. He could then see the quizzical look. "Kill for a bacon roll." He took the tablet from Owen and passed it across.

Brian was breathless and Cyril had already noticed the beads of sweat forming on his reddened forehead. Quickly picking up a paper napkin from one of the tables he handed it to him. It took a few moments for Brian to realise what it was for. He mopped his brow.

"Thanks."

"Run far?" Owen asked as he watched Brian wipe his face and then the back of his neck.

"No, must start some kind of training. I've let things slip recently what with…" He did not finish.

Owen interrupted. "Where was I before Eugene Bolt arrived?"

"Usain," Cyril corrected. "Please get on with it, Owen."

"Right, yes, Usain." Collecting his thoughts he studied his notes. "I believe the couple who checked out this morning are travelling north and will be staying in Richmond tonight. They are Martin and Emma Truelove."

Cyril raised an eyebrow. "Do you have their car registration number from the details left here when they checked in? I take it you've put out a call?" Cyril did not wait for an answer knowing if Owen had not, he soon would. "Brian, set out this room to interview those waiting in the lounge. The usual stuff and then get it uploaded. Did Kevin Carruthers return here on his own? I presume there will be CCTV in the entrance hall?" As Cyril spoke he instinctively popped his head through the door and scanned the hallway but could see no camera. He looked at the step plates strategically placed on the floor and the covering to the stairs positioned by the CSI in the hope of protecting any evidence there might be. Cyril was less optimistic than most. His experience had told him that collecting DNA from multi-use hotel-type facilities was akin to finding a needle in a haystack.

"I asked that question of the owner earlier. They couldn't say whether he returned alone or not and the only camera is the one on the wall outside. It faces the car park."

"Security? Apart from the small bell above the door that is." As he spoke, Cyril continued to look around the room before moving towards the window and then back to the door leading to the entrance.

"On an evening you need three keys to enter the property: the front door, the vestibule door, then a key to your own room. There's no sign of forced entry to any part of the building and all accommodation is on the first and second floors. There are two fire exits but they're still secured. They're also alarmed. You're given the keys on booking in."

"No card system?" Cyril questioned.

"I asked that but was told the costs are prohibitive for a small business."

"What if…" Cyril did not finish as he turned to see the doctor appear at the door to the breakfast room, his mask hung round his throat like a small hammock. The blue protective suit and shoes gave him a strange but positive air of authority.

"Cyril, not seen you for a while. How's Dr Pritchett?" He removed the glove to his right hand and tucked it under his arm before he thrust the warm and slightly sweaty palm in Cyril's direction.

"We're both well, thanks for asking." Cyril paused, hoping the pleasantries were concluded and he would find out more from the doctor about the body in the bed.

"Incised wounds… plural you note, Cyril. I'd say dead about twelve hours. The edges to the incisions are red, swollen and adherent with blood trace and lymph. However, if the neck injuries were the total damage it would suggest suicide at this stage but as yet there is no blade nor weapon… however, the post mortem removal of his right hand…"

Cyril said nothing but quickly looked at Owen realising now the significance of the smaller blood mark on the lower area of the sheet.

The doctor continued. "Interestingly we have incisions that are positioned above the thyroid." He paused and using his index finger touched Cyril's throat before running it almost horizontally. "Direction left to right. Multiple superficial and shallow wounds…"

"Hesitation cuts," Owen interrupted.

Both Cyril and the doctor looked at him briefly. The doctor smiled and nodded.

"Hesitation cuts, yes. There's tailing too to the wounds. We'll know more once he's back with the pathologist. If it's Dr Pritchett, Cyril, you'll be able to discuss it over cocoa." He winked at Owen and turned to leave.

"Owen, I was going to ask you something before the doctor arrived. Do you recall?"

Owen shook his head.

"Okay, if you two want to start the interviews. We also need to find his phone, assuming he has one, and do a check on his phone records. Last calls leading up to this convention and ideally we want to locate it as soon as."

***

The junction of Station Parade and the A61, York Place, was always busy and it was inevitable that traffic backed up across the short bridge spanning the twin track railway. However, on one side of the road was a wide grass verge and then the bridge balustrade. The railway lines ran below within the cutting, for some distance flanked on either side by The Stray. To the observer, the rails seemed to converge slowly into the distance below a second stone bridge that carried foot traffic from one side of The Stray to the other.

Apart from the abundance of rubbish that lay discarded along its entire length, four things caught the eye. The first was part of a broken bottle, refracting the sun's light, spreading not only the coloured spectrum across the dirt and the rail but also to the observer adding what seemed like some kind of coloured, fairy magic to a place that was not the prettiest. The observer's gaze lingered long until the sun disappeared taking with it the colours. The second item was a pram wheel and then a windscreen wiper arm and blade, the rubber split and spread like long, gnarled fingers. Lastly an object that resembled a yellow condom caught on what appeared to be a dead branch giving it the appearance of a small, limp pennant.

"Possibly a flag of victory," the observer whispered, the thought bringing with it an accompanying smile.

Within minutes three more items would join the detritus and they, it was hoped, would be left to settle and disappear within the stone ballast. The other two items, still wrapped in cling film, remained concealed for the moment. It would just be a matter of finding the right opportunity.

Chapter Four

Owen was now used to observing an autopsy. There were, during any of the latest procedures, fewer occasions when he needed to raise himself onto his toes to alleviate the on-coming signs of feeling light-headed and faint. He still, however, felt the beads of sweat run from his armpits and trickle cold against his skin but this was often brought on by the sounds, rather than the sights; the vibrating saw and drills as well as those created from the extraction of human organs. Although subtle, they seemed amplified for some reason and could quickly bring on a feeling of nausea. He watched and made notes as Dr Julie Pritchett, one of the north east pathologists, worked with her usual efficiency. Occasionally, her assistant, Hannah, would glance up and smile. Owen had been seeing Hannah for some time. He remembered their initial meeting and his clumsy first advances. He had not considered that she was already in a relationship when he invited her to meet for a drink. Her initial refusal had hit him harder than he imagined.

***

The Mercedes Actros wagon, parked in the designated area, was the opportunity to lose another item, another piece of evidence. He had not expected the opportunity to arise so soon but one could not look a gift horse in the mouth. The curtains in the cab were drawn, another advantage. Either the driver was sleeping or not in the cab. The registration plate denoted the wagon was a long way from home; it was Romanian and therefore it was an even greater bonus. Following a quick look round, the owner of the gloved hand swiftly removed the fuel tank filler on the tractor unit. Looking into the opening, the observer was relieved to see there was no fixed filter. One never could tell from the outside. Quickly removing the cling film, he dropped the secateurs through the opening into the cavernous fourteen hundred litre tank.

"Perfect! Now when and where will you be discovered I wonder, if at all?" The top was replaced and the glove removed, turning it inside out in the process. It was then tucked under the rear of the trailer to be thrown off on some road like so many other odd gloves. Now the fun could begin with the strategic disposal of the final object.

***

Cyril stared at the computer screen clearly showing the cover of the pathologist's report. He allowed his fingers to drum on the desk as he organised his thoughts knowing only too well the report's contents. He lifted the china cup from the saucer and sipped his tea before reading the cover details again as he focused on the name, Dr Julie Pritchett, bringing with it a comforting warmth. It was getting more difficult for him to see her in her professional role. He stopped tapping and allowed his finger to run under her name as if in a gentle caress. "You're getting maudlin, Bennett, come on." He moved the mouse and her name vanished leaving the first page and the descriptive notes and images.

Although the incisions were characteristically those of suicidal cut-throat wounds, it seemed this death was anything but. Clear medical evidence suggested that Mr Kevin Carruthers had died painfully and slowly. There was confirmation the hand amputation was performed after death, hence the minimal blood loss in that area. It was, however, the damage to the neck that drew Cyril's attention. Each cut had been deliberate and controlled until the final incision. Cyril looked more closely at the images and referenced them to the report. He followed the incision from the head of the wound with his finger. There had been minute slivers of coloured glass found within parts of the flesh to the edge of the wounds suggesting the weapon used in the attack was some kind of honed glass, but exactly what shape or type, could not be determined at this stage.

The light in the room dimmed as Owen stood in the doorway.

"You'd make a better door than a window, Owen. Have you read the pathologist's report?"

Owen moved towards the desk, a *Harrogate Festival* mug gripped firmly in his right hand and a custard cream in his left. Cyril was relieved and surprised that the outer rim of the mug was not awash with tea.

"I was present if you recall, sir. It seems that all the recent autopsies have my name on them these days. Tortured, silently tortured if that's not an oxymoron and then…"

Cyril turned to look at his colleague, startled by his use of such a literary term. Owen brought the biscuit to his throat and ran it across whilst pulling a facial expression that conveyed terror. It brought a smile to Cyril's lips.

"Still have the skills you learned treading the boards, I see, plus a growing understanding of the Queen's English." There was no sarcasm in his words.

"I've had a few nights on the tiles but can't remember treading on any boards and I can swear with the best of them. Being brought up in Bradford and working in Bradford Vice Division you hear it all." Owen popped the whole biscuit into his mouth.

"A one off! I rest my case, Owen, I rest my case."

"How come no one heard? The walls in these B&Bs aren't too soundproof. There must've been some kind of struggle. No weapon, so he can't have killed himself, then chopped off his hand before hiding that and the tools used. There was no forcing of any of the locks, so either the killer was taken in or he was already there when Carruthers returned."

"Or she."

"Or she? Yes… Possible. Although he's not a big lad he looks young enough and fit enough to defend himself so for a woman to hold him, torture him and then..." Owen was just about to cut his throat again with his finger but on seeing Cyril's expression thought better of it. "Remember according to the report he was found naked, no evidence of sexual activity and no signs of a struggle. When you see Dr Pritchett, you might ask what her personal thoughts are on the death." He paused for a moment. "We're checking those known to the police from the people attending and working at the convention."

"Phone, Owen?"

"Nothing in the room nor with his clothes. We have a log from his provider of his last calls and we're checking those. Names will be with us shortly. Since the death the phone has been deactivated."

"Par for the course. Any info from the guests staying at *The Grey House*?"

***

Valerie buttered the toast ensuring it spread to the very edges before slicing diagonally. She had once heard that this was the way toast should be sliced and from that point on, she had followed this etiquette. She had always followed rules from being a child and by doing so she had usually got her own way. She was not particularly academic and school was something she endured before leaving early to work in sales in a large department store.

She removed her linen napkin from the silver holder. It had been her mother's and before that, possibly her grandmother's. Regardless, it connected her with her past each day at meal times and it brought a degree of reassurance. Nibbling her toast she reflected on the previous evening and the momentary pause allowed the liquefied butter to drizzle onto the plate she held on her lap.

The evening had been as she had imagined. They had strolled along the edge of The Stray before ending up at *The Old Swan Hotel*. She had had it in her mind to go there from the outset, liking the ambience and its old-world charm. Leaning forward she touched the napkin ring again.

It was during the second drink that she had heard it in his accent. "You said you were from Yorkshire but I detect that may not be the whole truth," she had whispered. Her sentence was neither threatening nor defensive and she deliberately chuckled and put a hand on his knee as she said it, to remove the possibility of any offence. As he laughed she removed her hand, its job had been done and therefore no longer necessary at this stage. She did not want to convey the wrong impression; this was after all, their first date. She had, however, been correct. He had lived most of his early years in Hexham. Private schooling and elocution lessons had wiped away much of a regional accent but there was, to the discerning ear, the odd clue detectible in certain sounds.

She finished her toast, washed the knife and plate before feeding Monty. "Will he ring and ask me out again?" she asked the cat as it wrapped itself around her legs and mewed affectionately. "You're not sure are you, and neither am I. There aren't too many fish in the sea these days, Monty."

The cat seemed to respond to the word *fish* and jumped on her recently vacated chair.

"You are a clever pussy."

Within half an hour she would be back at the charity shop.

***

An officer had taken a statement from Emma and Martin Truelove. He had traced their car to Richmond and they had been fully co-operative. They had neither seen nor knew Carruthers. "They only stayed one night and seeing he didn't have breakfast…" Owen stopped as Cyril raised his hand.

"The others?"

Owen became quite animated as he underlined two names written on a flipchart that was positioned on an easel to the side of Cyril's desk. "This couple have been staying at *The*

Grey House for the last two nights; they should be leaving in a few days. They'd booked in the same day as the dead man and were also attending the convention."

"Has their room been checked by Forensics?" Cyril interrupted, suddenly more interested. "Anyone who was in the building could have killed him. All we need is evidence, scientific if possible, and a motive. That's always helpful." He brought his hand up to his forehead and rubbed.

"A hand too would help! Forensics is checking each room. Their room," he tapped the underlined names, "by coincidence, it's next door to that occupied by Carruthers and as I said, sir, this couple, Daniel Frost and Ruth Bishop, are both gamers."

"Just pause a moment, Owen, and let's take stock. Sit down and tell me what we know about this convention."

Owen smiled inwardly at the royal *we*. He remembered Cyril once saying that only kings, presidents and people with tapeworms should use the word in that sense but he could not remember who had originally said it; Cyril had told him and so he made sure it was exaggerated when he spoke. "*We* know a lot, as *we* checked their website."

Cyril did not allow his face to slip at Owen's sarcasm.

"It's a mixture of predominantly board and card games. There are a few computer games but not many. The common theme for this event is to get people to sit and interact. They can borrow from a vast library of games if they have a Game Passport. They pay a refundable deposit to receive one and then borrow a game and go and play. As you're aware, the centre is a bloody big place and can cater for hundreds. There are seminars where tactics and game play are discussed in detail. They present strategic moves and explain rule application. Experts, and in some cases the designers, of a particular game or genre of game hold seminars where tactics…"

"And the type of games?"

"*Fuji Flush, Cottage Garden, Virus, Chromosome, Undercover, Burke's Gambit*. I could go on."

Cyril rubbed his forehead again as if searching for some inspiration or understanding. "Not exactly cricket is it? How competitive are these games?"

"I've checked out a few. Let me tell you about two to begin with. Firstly, *Burke's Gambit*. Like many, it's a social deduction game to do with a parasite and infection. The rules, from what I can make out, seem overly complicated so I've given the task to Harry to look into and hopefully interpret them. However, they all have a similar theme and that can be death or instant death depending on the way the cards or the dice fall. Some even have a traitor or two lurking within the players."

"A bit like real life!" Cyril said, the tone of his words carrying sincerity.

"Indeed. In the second game, *Chromosome*, people start dying after a meteor lands bringing with it deadly microbes. Slowly everyone is eliminated and the idea of the game is finally to kill the germs before they get the last man standing who is one of the players."

"Or last woman, Owen? I don't like the plural you speak of... People start dying. The one we have at the moment is quite enough."

"Diversity rules, sir, sorry. The last woman!"

"Another game, but that one's political, Owen."

"Just one of today's facts of life but please don't get me started on diversity for..." He did not finish as his face started to flush.

Cyril fully understood Owen's feelings on the subject and that of the positive discrimination within the force where promotion was concerned; it was, to Owen, a raw and exposed nerve.

"Being a single white male can be a positive disadvantage these days that's all I'm saying otherwise I'll turn bitter and twisted." There was a momentary pause. "So... you feel Carruthers may well have lost his life by losing a game?" Owen responded not realising the significance.

"Maybe, Owen, maybe. Do we know the games he played whilst there?"

"We're checking to see if he had a Game Passport. I'm assuming there should be some kind of register as money is involved. We've put his photograph on the various sites and that should hopefully bring contacts of those who played the games with him during his time there. It's just a case of waiting for the pieces to drop into place. There's also a chance that many of those at the event have been to other similar games conventions or been involved in local games nights. I'm guessing but it's probably a possibility."

Cyril checked his watch. Owen waited for him to shake it but he was to be disappointed. "Get Harry and Brian to feed back tomorrow morning. Get Shakti to look at as many of the games as possible. Get her to liaise with Harry, two heads are better than one, and talk to the organisers, they may know him if he's a regular. If we can tie certain games to Carruthers, we might be a little closer to determining a reason he was killed." Cyril stood.

"If it's anything to do with the games and the convention at all, that is."

Owen's words made Cyril frown.

"Another reason? Thanks for that, Owen. Great!"

"The couple whose names I underlined before you asked about the gaming convention, sir? You might be interested to know that they identified him standing in the grounds of what was St Luke's church. They thought it was still a church, but as you know, it was converted into apartments some time back. Interestingly, he wasn't alone. They believe that he could have been with a woman."

Cyril sat down again, suddenly interested. "Any CCTV there or on King's Road?"

"Checking all known cameras from the centre to that building."

"Keep me informed. Well done!" Cyril checked his watch again. "Home. Just organise a briefing for eight tomorrow morning and set up an incident room. I think this case will not be as simple as first thought. And Owen, I remembered what I was thinking when at *The Grey House*. What if a guest goes off with the three keys? I've done it in the past on more than one occasion."

"They probably post them back. They have a huge brass ball on them, it's unlikely they'd walk off with that."

"Trust me, Owen, it's easily done. Check, please." Cyril collected his belongings and went to the door. "And Owen, don't forget to take your mug when you leave. Hearing what microbes and parasites can do worries my sensitivities and looking at the state of the internal surface of your drinking vessel one can never be too careful." He winked at his colleague and started to leave. "See you tomorrow."

"Sir. Did you not find the evidence from the nail scrapes interesting?"

Cyril paused in the doorway as if waiting for the punchline.

Owen moved to the screen, tucking his tie into his shirt to keep it from the keyboard before his fingers danced on the keys below adding his own password. "Here it is. I remember Dr Pritchett cutting the nails for exogenous cell recovery, which is standard procedure as you know, just in case the attacker's DNA was under the nails. However, she did find a long splinter and from the physical evidence and the colouration of the surrounding tissue she felt it hadn't been there too long. You can see it here in the photographs and during extraction. It's gone for testing along with the cells. As she said during the autopsy, it could have happened at any time in the last few days and have nothing to do with the case."

Cyril came across, popped on his glasses and looked at the images as Owen identified the key elements from the text and photographs. "You'll be chasing that I take it?"

"In hand... no pun intended." He simply looked at Cyril.

Chapter Five

The breeze channelled through the gap between the buildings, the Venturi effect accelerating the travelling air which Cyril immediately sensed as he turned to head down the narrow passageway towards Robert Street. It brought with it a marked change in temperature. It never ceased to surprise Cyril and always led him to reminisce, taking him back to when he was learning to fly. He paused briefly. Those were fun days he had often thought, days when his head was more in the clouds than on his work. His shifts then always seemed so carefree, the weather warmer, people more friendly and crimes less sadistic and cruel. The policing did not seem as sophisticated either, it was more exciting and certainly less bureaucratic and there were more officers on the beat. He chuckled to himself thinking he sounded just like his father had done when he was young. Maybe the best days were behind him and that would never do. Probably the sense of freedom brought with learning to fly had offered him a halcyon view of the past. Alas, those days were long gone.

The sun had seemed warm as he crossed The Stray but now, removing his head from the memory clouds, he shivered but not for long. On coming out on the other side of the passageway, a matter of fifteen strides, he felt again the warm caress of the sun strike the side of his face. He was immediately back in the present.

Having just put the key in the door lock he heard his name called.

"Mr Bennett."

The high-pitched, questioning, female voice rang out across the street and there was no denying its Germanic edge.

"Mr Bennett?"

Cyril turned, recognising the accent and the timbre. He felt a sigh rise in his throat. It was one of his neighbours. Mrs Pfeiffer had lived opposite since he had moved in. She knew everyone's business, and although that was often a drawback when Julie came to the house guaranteeing the certainty of flickering net curtains, she was also the best security the street enjoyed.

"Mr Bennett, I'm glad you've arrived home before I take Hercule for his walk."

As if on cue, the Dachshund began to bark and peer out from between her swollen ankles. Cyril looked at the brown-coated dog as he dutifully crossed the street before opening the gate. Hercule immediately bolted between Mrs Pfeiffer's legs and greeted Cyril by rolling over before wriggling and slithering for maximum attention.

"Now Badger Hound, I can't see you tackling a big, bad brock, you old softy." Cyril rubbed the dog's belly as it wriggled furiously with excitement. A small whimper of pleasure matched the movements perfectly.

"He's always liked you, Mr Bennett. If only he were the same with the milkman and the postman. When your parcel was delivered he went like one of those missiles, you know the ones, to attack him and I'm not as fast as I used to be. One day he'll catch the lad."

Cyril turned to look at her and he could see the frown on her face.

"Ballistic?" Cyril proffered.

"Yes, yes. Ballistic. You'd never guess that I've lived here longer than I lived in Stuttgart, would you?"

It was true. She still had a pronounced accent. On hearing the word 'parcel' Cyril's stomach fluttered, an excitement borne on the anticipation of the contents.

"You'll have to get it if old softy there will let you stop. It's rather heavy." She paused hoping that Cyril would divulge what the contents might be but he resisted. If he had relented, he realised that everyone in the street would also know so he simply smiled.

"A present," he lied as he approached the door. The smell of cooking leaked through the opening. It was not an unpleasant smell and it made his stomach rumble.

"It's just by the settee."

***

Within fifteen minutes Cyril had opened the bulky parcel. It was more like stripping a Russian doll; after taking off one layer of packaging there was yet another beneath. Now, however, he sat and stared at the item he had removed from the wrapping. The bronze abstract figure stood on the table. *Solitary Man* by John Coen.

Cyril had been checking the auction sites and had seen this lot for sale in Ireland with a realistic estimate. Before he knew it he had bid for it on the telephone and won. That was two weeks ago. Running his hand over the cold bronze he was delighted with his purchase. In a few months he would sell it on at a local auction, hopefully at a profit. He felt the excitement grow. He would like to make a killing. How he loved this game.

Chapter Six

The incident room looked a little bare. There was none of the magical interactive screens that could zoom from one part of the town to the other whilst tracking the suspect, or mysteriously interpreting the evidence as seen on many television dramas of such procedures. To the untrained eye the room would simply be classed as disappointing and a little underwhelming. On one wall was a collection of photographs of the deceased, above the notes that had been on Cyril's easel the day before. There was also a large flat computer screen on the far wall, the blue and white glow from the North Yorkshire Police logo screensaver casting a cold sheen onto the white walls of the room. The day would see a greater, concentrated build-up of evidence as more forensic results came in. Witness statements, although now handled and cross-referenced digitally, would still need analysing.

DC Harry Nixon, DC Brian Smirthwaite, DC Shakti Misra and April Richmond, now a DS after successfully completing a fast-track promotional course aimed specifically to support female and ethnic minority officers within the ranks, chatted as Cyril entered.

"Morning," Cyril said in his normal positive and upbeat fashion. He received a similar response that was totally in concert. "Just hanging on for Owen, he'll only be a moment."

As if on cue Owen entered carrying a small file. He let it fall onto the table before removing his jacket and loosening his tie. He glanced at Cyril who nodded and looked at his watch.

"Left my brew, sir." Owen looked optimistically in the hope Cyril would suggest he go and retrieve it but he was disappointed. He took a moment to organise himself and as he looked up, those chatting stopped.

"Kevin James Carruthers, twenty-nine years old. Lived in Leyburn and had done for the past three years. His address and details are here." Owen dealt out the sheets of paper as if passing out playing cards. He gave them a moment to peruse them. "As far as we know he wasn't in a relationship and lived in a one bedroomed flat, new one too. Previous to that he had lived in rented accommodation."

"We have those details?"

"Checking."

"Relatives and family?" April asked.

"Checking. We do know he was a funeral director from a conversation I had with the owner of *The Grey House* and that's been confirmed. Name and address there too." Owen looked up waiting to take any questions.

"Why stay over for the event, what is it... an hour's drive between Leyburn and Harrogate?" Cyril asked, aware that the deceased had checked in to the bed and breakfast accommodation for the extended period of the event.

"It might not seem far but the man didn't have a driver's licence and I think, more specifically, a lot of what goes on at these conventions takes place in the evening," Owen explained.

"An undertaker not being able to drive?"

"He might be the one that walks at the front wearing the top hat," Harry Nixon suggested not meaning to be funny but it made Owen giggle.

April immediately looked up and frowned bringing back the focus. "Evening games? Extracurricular games in the true sense or is there a suspicion of something else?"

Cyril liked April, he had done since she had joined the team. He thought Liz Graydon would be a hard act to follow but she had been more than a match for the challenges they had faced. She was quick to ask and even quicker to act. She had a keen sense of humour but she was also a consummate professional and knew just what lines could not be crossed. And now he had a fear that with the new promotion she would not be with him long. There was talk of a swift rise to the rank of Inspector and if that were to happen he could see a degree of resentment festering within other officers who did not meet the new diversification criteria.

"From what I can tell they play late into the night and well after the event closes. They meet either in hotels or pubs. Many of the larger hotels have lounges and they continue there, even when having a meal some of the gamers don't stop."

April spoke again. "We have CCTV footage of Carruthers leaving the Convention Centre with a group of three others, two men and a woman at about 20.15. They were then seen again on CCTV heading up Parliament Street and also at the Cenotaph. We can find nothing else after that but we're still trawling."

"What's your guess?" Cyril asked as he inspected his e-cigarette before tucking it back into the breast pocket of his jacket.

"One of the hotels along Prospect Place? There are three." April named them.

"You're checking?"

"As we speak. We also know from the display boards…" she directed her hand to point to the list of names Owen had underlined but did not take her eyes off the group. "…it's been alleged but not yet confirmed that he was seen standing in or around St Luke's apartments by the couple whose names are underlined and who were staying at *The Grey House.* From questioning some attendees we know that people living in or close to Harrogate still participate in these games so it's worth remembering that one of those with Carruthers that night might have an apartment there or close by." She looked up anticipating Cyril's next question. "As we speak, sir. So, we need to know his whereabouts between 20.15 and the approximate time of his death around midnight." Owen was making notes accompanied by doodles as she spoke.

"20.35 was the last known confirmed sighting but the unofficial and unconfirmed sighting leaves us with a one hour window. As the church is within five minutes' walk of his accommodation, we're looking at a missing fifty-five minutes. How did he get from the area around the Cenotaph to St Luke's without being seen on CCTV? And if my map reading is as good as I think it is, being seen there, at St Luke's, means he was meeting someone or he'd have returned to his digs using a shorter and more convenient route."

"Brian, what about that couple… Frost and Bishop who coincidentally were sleeping in the next room to Carruthers?" Cyril asked as he inadvertently mimicked April and pointed to the two names underlined on the board. "You interviewed them and according to Owen, they were also gamers."

"Yes, very co-operative they were too. They'd been playing in the bar area of the Crowne Plaza with another couple. They left at about 22.30. The couple with whom they were playing were staying there. They walked back to *The Grey House* and it was then they believe they saw Carruthers."

"What made them notice him? Surely it was dark and the grounds of the building are higher than the road if I recall correctly?" April asked as she leaned closer.

"According to Bishop it was the laugh. One of the two suddenly burst out laughing and it startled them; it had been quiet walking up King's Road apart from the occasional car and they weren't expecting it. Both Frost and Bishop turned to look in the direction of the laughter. They believe it was Carruthers once they'd seen the photograph of the deceased. They realised they'd seen him before on the two previous days, at breakfast and once at the convention so they knew him by sight. I presumed it must have been dark. There are trees and there is some raised garden between the pavement and the building but they said not; the face of the one looking towards the road was clearly visible."

There was a pause as a number of the officers made jottings on the paper Owen had passed to them.

"Let me try to understand this. So, from wherever they went at the top of Parliament Street, Carruthers found his way to a rendezvous by the apartments either alone or with one of those seen or someone else?" Cyril asked.

"That's what it seems like so far. We need to know where he went after the sighting," April responded with a degree of impatience in her tone.

Sensing her irritation Owen quickly moved on. "I take it you've all read the pathology report. We've added a number of photographs to the boards. The weapon used looks like a piece of glass. I'm told that by cutting glass in a certain way you can achieve an angled and extremely sharp edge. However, it's so fine that it's inevitable it will leave some traces, minute, almost invisible slivers as it cuts, and in this case, those were found embedded along three of the cuts. Our killer must've known that they'd be there and also that they'd be found. According to the forensic results more than one piece of glass was used. The hand amputation they believe was done using some type of secateurs."

"Do we know the origin of the glass... colour, type or age?" Shakti asked, her pencil sitting on her lower lip, the tip quite heavily chewed.

Owen turned to Cyril.

"What I've been able to ascertain from the experts, but more work has to be done, is that the glass is probably old and coloured. According to them it's red, possibly antique as there are traces of gold salts that are used in the process of colouring glass, especially cranberry coloured glass. Each sliver is also from the same sheet as they consistently show the same refractive index according to the GRIM." He paused watching a few frowns appear. "It's kind of appropriate, I do like that acronym. That, as you know, stands for the Glass Refracted Index Measurement. The glass was carried in some protective sheath probably leather, to protect the carrier. There were no traceable contaminants, apart from gun oil residue."

The word *gun* made a number of officers look directly at Cyril.

"Don't get excited. I'm informed the wheels used for glass cutting are lubricated with a fine oil and even though, as I said, the glass had been cleaned, there was still a trace."

"The pruning clippers, anything there?" Brian continued to doodle as he asked the question.

"Forensics are looking at traces of metal left on the bone fragments and that should show something in time but I'm assured they were new. There was also a wooden splinter found under the thumb of his left hand. Forensics thought that this had occurred fairly recently and that proved to be the case, two or three days max. It was pine, unpainted but there was evidence of plaster of Paris within the sample."

"New apartment, rubbing down some of the woodwork to add a bit of colour? You know how clinical new builds can be," Harry suggested.

"That's also to be investigated. It's all about when he received the injury."

"So, as we sit here, we have people looking through the records of those attending the event. They're checking Carruthers's friends, relatives and work colleagues. We're then going to try to piece together his whereabouts not only whilst in Harrogate, but in the days, weeks and if necessary, the months leading up to his death. Your job is to keep abreast of what's coming in and put the pieces together… that is, if the computers don't do that before you. Anything else before Owen dashes to see if his brew is still drinkable?"

"Phone records are in and those numbers who called and were called are being checked. Should have a list in forty-eight hours," Shakti stated as she shuffled the papers in front of her. "I'll add them to the system and the boards when they come in."

Cyril nodded. "Banking details, money, anything unusual about his accounts? Let's look. Anything else?"

"One other thing." It was Owen's turn to stop everyone from moving. "Harry and Shakti have been looking into the types of games played at the convention, particularly those that were borrowed using a Game Passport. April, if you'd liaise with them and see if there's anything relevant, threatening… anything that might be worth following up. Is the lost hand significant apart from the obvious? I don't want someone to tell me he had a bad hand or that he chucked in his hand." Owen did not give them time to react. "Referencing all the players who used the same games might open up a lead to be pursued. Right now, that's a proverbial needle in a haystack. 8.20. There's work to be done."

Chapter Seven

8.40 in the morning and the thought of a drive to Leyburn filled Cyril with dread as he searched his desk drawers for the packet of travel sickness tablets he knew were there somewhere. *Call yourself a bloody detective and you can't even find...* He stopped as his hand rested on the familiar pack of tablets and he suddenly felt relieved. Motion sickness in boats, buses and cars had always plagued him especially as a child. Surprisingly, he found he could stomach flying, probably because of the exhilaration. He was fine too when he drove but with Owen at the wheel it was always a lottery.

It had to be said that the route took them through some stunning scenery and he could see why Yorkshire was referred to as *God's own country.* Crossing the River Ure at Masham, Cyril glanced to his right catching a glimpse of the Black Sheep Brewery. He dropped the window a fraction in the hope of smelling the rich aroma that often lingered in the air. Beer making from the two breweries situated in the centre of the small town often filled the atmosphere with a rich pungency that some people loved and others hated. Alas, today it evaded him. His phone rang.

"Bennett." He listened keeping his eyes on the twisting road ahead.

"No relatives living close. Older brother, Richard, lives in Hornby." DC Stuart Park tried to tell him its location and should have known better. "I know where it is, yes. Occupation?" Cyril glanced at Owen. "A what? Thanks."

"Undertaker like his brother?" Owen asked whilst glancing sideways, trying to predict Cyril's answer.

"You'd never guess. A Shooting Ground Administrator and Receptionist."

Owen frowned. "Come again?"

"I kid you not."

"What's that when it's at home?"

"A posh name for someone who looks after a clay pigeon shoot, I'm led to believe."

"One brother kills and the other brother buries, now that's what I call teamwork."

Cyril quickly turned to look at Owen. "Many a true word, my friend."

Owen drove up Mightens Bank just as they approached Leyburn before turning right. Cyril checked his watch and shook his wrist before looking again. He had always wanted a Rolex and this he had bought as a special fortieth birthday present to himself, a reward. He had always wanted the Explorer 2 model. The words, *Superlative Chronometer* written on the face and its rugged design had attracted him. Why he shook it was a mystery to his colleagues but it was something he always did, a bit like a nervous tic.

"It's just along here on the right." Cyril pointed in the general direction.

Owen turned off the road into a courtyard for the small collection of apartments and houses. He parked up.

"Number 13A. After this visit it's the undertakers in Richmond to see a Mr Duffers. They're expecting us this morning."

"*Duffers' Funerals,*" Owen said between giggles. "I'd have a lot of confidence in them!"

"*Nature's Call* Funeral Directors. Behave, Owen."

"If he lived here and worked in Richmond and he didn't drive, how the hell did he get there? It has to be twelve miles and I bet the buses aren't that frequent."

"That's something I suspect we'll find out later. All in good time."

Cyril removed a plastic bag from his pocket and looked at the set of keys the CSI had retrieved from the dead man's room at the B&B. They had been cleared by Forensics as a matter of urgency. Fortunately, he did not need to look for the correct flat as an officer was standing outside the door to the apartment block. It had been at Cyril's request. Once news spread of a death it was open season for petty crooks to seize the opportunity.

***

Wendy Momen walked along Cornwall Road approaching the Sun Pavilion as she did most days. Normally she would have been earlier but today was her day off and it gave her more time to walk her dog, Trixi. The lazy start also suited her. Although she was following her usual route and had a tendency to meet the same people along the way, today would be different. After walking through the park it was her habit to stroll into town, get a coffee and maybe a cake before home. Her husband, Bill, would be out all day at the fine art gallery he owned and ran.

The signs positioned on the lamp posts clearly requested dogs be kept on the lead. She complied although that was not always the case with other owners she had noticed, but then nothing seemed to be done. She was soon standing by the old Magnesia Well pump room, a small structure that seemed to bring to mind the fairy stories she had read as a child. In some ways it was one of her special places. She could imagine it made of gingerbread with its sweeping, ornate eaves and small paned, arched windows that appeared to hold hands with the door that sat equally spaced between. They were to her, the Father, the Son and the Holy Ghost. There was something about their religious architectural design quality and their symmetry. Even though she was here most days, she always stopped to admire it, to check like a proud guardian. The dog strained at the leash, eager to continue the walk. She allowed the lead to extend and the dog disappeared into the shrubbery whilst she admired the roof. For the first time she noticed that the tiles followed a similar pattern to the front of the building. Trixi growled and barked once before returning. It was only then she saw it.

***

Both men had slipped on plastic overshoes and gloves before entering. The stairs to the first floor apartment were carpeted. Cyril slipped the key into the lock, opened the door and waited for the alarm to remind him it needed a code but there was nothing.

The entrance hall was small with just a table, a lamp and a mirror. They walked to the first door. Elegantly framed posters advertising games were hung on the walls. The room was clean, ordered and extremely tidy.

"He lives here on his own?" Owen asked as he looked along one of the glass coffee tables for dust. "A bit like my gaff!"

Cyril immediately laughed. "Chalk and cheese, Owen."

"Being this tidy is the sign of a sick mind if you ask me. You have to have a bit of dirt in your life to keep the immune system functioning fully." Owen's tone suggested there was some admiration for Carruthers.

Cyril said nothing but continued to look around the room. The far wall was furnished with a number of shelves, each containing boxes of games. He tilted his head sideways and read the titles, *City of Iron, Dead of Winter, Rockwell.* He stopped at one, *Chromosome,* allowing his covered finger to rest on the shelf below. "This is the game you talked about, Owen, the last man standing. Remember?"

Owen approached and tilted his head in order to read the title. "Yes, that's the one."

"Photograph the shelves so that we can see immediately if there are any games here that he played whilst at the convention."

Cyril's phone rang again. He fumbled in his pocket but the protective gloves made it difficult to retrieve it. Once the phone was out he tried to answer but with the surgical glove it proved impossible. Owen had slipped off his glove and took the phone. He pressed for speaker.

"Thanks, Owen."

"Bennett," Owen said mimicking the way his boss answered the phone.

"It's April, Owen. Is *Flash* there?"

"It's on speaker."

"Sorry! Right. We have another body." She deliberately paused as she heard the two men speak together.

"What?"

"Where?"

"There are too many similarities to Carruthers's case for it to be a coincidence. Thought you should know immediately. The doctor and Forensics are on their way as he wasn't discovered until 11.00."

"Who found the body?" Cyril asked leaning closer to the phone.

"Cleaner, as in the last case. Found at *The Victorian Guest House,* just off East Parade, not too far from *The Grey House*. They believe he was also at the convention but they sounded confused."

"Get over there and report as soon as."

"I'm there now… Harry's with me. We'll close it down and follow the set procedures… Just a minute… The Doctor and CSI are here now so should know more soon."

"Patch us in to any images and details as you get them." Owen hung up. "Serial killer or coincidence?"

"She thinks the former from her tone but it could simply be a heart attack. Let's not cross too many bridges until we have the facts. We need to get this checked and then on to the undertakers. What worries me is our lack of manpower. This government thinks we go about helping folk across the bloody road when we don't have enough officers to cope with serious crime!"

"Don't forget investigating those who upset others, the so-called hate crimes."

Cyril's facial expression said it all. "Do not get me bloody started, Owen, not now!"

***

Wendy tried to focus on the protruding area of the roof. Hanging from one of the triangular openings within the eaves was what looked to be an inflated rubber glove. Moving closer, Wendy could see that the fist was closed. She stretched up but it was out of reach. "Well, that's a first, Trixi." Her curiosity getting the better of her, she looked around and found a short stick. The dog barked optimistically hoping it would be thrown. She tugged the lead before raising the stick towards the glove. Now she could touch it, which she did, delicately at first. "It's not a glove, well at least not a latex one." She pushed a little harder. The dog still wanted her to throw the stick and danced at her feet offering the occasional encouraging bark. That immediately turned into a yelp as the hand dropped, striking the dog just behind the right ear. It made Wendy jump too and she dropped the stick. Trixi moved towards it and sniffed but was quickly pulled away.

"Leave it!" The dog moved back to her feet.

Wendy looked around conscious that this might be some huge prank, one that was being filmed to be added to social media. She hoped that nobody would open the door pointing a camera into her startled face. From what she could see there was only one man in the area but he was too far away to be involved. The sound of the distant traffic continued as normal. Retrieving the stick she bravely prodded the object, rotating it on the flagstone. The formed fist remained tight. It certainly looked real. She shuddered. Now she had a dilemma. Should she phone the police and report *I've found a hand in the park* and when they come it turns out to be made of rubber? She could just hear the sarcasm in some young bobby's retort. *It's latex, madam, thanks for wasting our valuable time.* Maybe it would be better to phone Bill. He could be there in ten minutes or maybe she should just walk away as if she had discovered nothing.

She decided that was the most sensible if not the most responsible action to take but then as she was leaving she saw a mother with a young child. The last thing she wanted was for a child to find it. The decision was made. She rang Bill.

45

***

Most things in the flat seemed in order. They found a laptop and an electronic tablet. "Hopefully the tech people will be able to get a good deal from these. Have we checked his social media pages?"

"In the process, sir."

"Right, the undertakers and then a swift ride back." Cyril knew that with blue lights and a siren on the unmarked car he would be the colour of grass when he finally returned to Harrogate. He took another *Qwell*.

***

Bill arrived more quickly than Wendy anticipated. Trixi barked on seeing him appear. He hugged his wife. "Where is it?"

"I pushed it under that shrub with the stick just in case a child or a dog appeared."

Bill looked at her in tune with what she was thinking. "And ran off with it?"

She nodded.

"That's good thinking." He lifted the foliage cautiously before bending down like a man about to confront an unidentifiable poisonous snake.

Wendy stood some distance away and watched as her husband's facial expression changed from one of intrigue and uncertainty to one of sheer horror.

"It's real." In one motion he put his hand to his mouth and turned away to look at Wendy. He took out his phone.

Chapter Eight

Cyril and Owen had just crossed the bridge coming into Richmond and as usual the castle attracted Cyril's attention.

"Simply stunning, Owen. Never get tired of this town…" He did not finish his sentence as his phone rang. He let it ring a couple of times as he exhaled a long sigh. "Is nothing sacred?"

"Bennett."

"It's Shakti, sir. Thought you needed to know immediately. Carruthers's hand has been located. Found by a member of the public, a Wendy Momen."

Cyril immediately thought of his stepmother, the Wendy he had allowed back into his life after the death of his father and for a brief moment he was distracted. "Sorry, where?"

Shakti went through the details.

"If you hear anything from the lab let me know immediately. Forensics are at the scene now I take it?" He listened attentively glancing occasionally at Owen.

"One more thing, twenty-six thousand pounds was withdrawn from his account the day before his body was discovered. The transaction had been arranged two days previously."

"Do we know why?"

"We believe it has something to do with the flat. It's a cash withdrawal."

Cyril pulled a face, thanked Shakti before returning the phone to his pocket.

"The hand is no longer missing, Owen. Found stuffed in a hole in the eaves of Magnesia Well in the Valley Gardens."

He saw a puzzled look appear on Owen's face. "You know, the small building?"

"No, sir… Eaves?"

"The wooden frontage of the roof, the bit that overhangs. Obviously whoever put it there wanted to keep it off the ground away from rats and other vermin that would make short work of it. It never rains but it pours, Owen. Just think of the costs of this little lot!"

Owen had noticed over the last six months or so just how much Cyril worried over the financing of the investigations and wondered whether his regular visits to the North Yorkshire Police Headquarters and to the Chief Constable up in Northallerton were adding unacceptable pressure to his already difficult job. He made a mental note to have a word with Julie. It was not that long ago Cyril considered packing it all in after the death of Liz Graydon. He looked across at his boss realising just how lucky he was to work with someone with the dedication and professionalism that Cyril held so dear.

"Speaking of costs, Carruthers withdrew a large amount in cash prior to his death but it's believed to have something to do with the flat."

"Sounds reasonable. And sir, remember we can only do what we can with the resources we have available. We don't perform miracles, not on my salary at any rate."

Cyril said nothing but it did bring the hint of a smile.

***

The *Nature's Call* undertaker's building was situated within a small and elegant cobbled courtyard. Two large, arched doors were obviously the garages for their vehicles. It was difficult to determine the original use of the structure but they might well have been the coaching house and stables of a larger property.

They were greeted by an elderly receptionist, who, on looking at Cyril's ID, understood the real nature of his visit. She nodded, her face sombre. "You're expected, Detective Chief

Inspector, please take a seat. Mr Duffers will be with you shortly."

The quiet background music that seemed to drift like the scent from the diffuser on the edge of the desk was somehow more soothing than he had anticipated. Normally it would have irritated but today Cyril felt himself relax for the first time since finishing his walk to work, and that seemed like hours ago.

"It's hard to believe, Mr Bennett, that last week he was sitting right where you are now, poor man, and next week he may well be next door in our chapel of rest. One can never take anything in this life for granted. One just never knows." Duffers clasped his hands together inadvertently creating a steeple with his fingers.

Cyril shuffled in the dead man's seat now feeling decidedly uncomfortable. "How long has he worked for you?"

"Five years. He came after serving an apprenticeship at the Co-op, but I can check if you want a precise answer. Very good mortician and sensitive embalmer but his true skill was in presentation. He could really transform…"

Cyril interrupted. Those details he neither wanted to hear nor needed. "What do you know about him… his social life, Mr Duffers?"

"One thing we all found strange was that he didn't have a television, played games a lot and studied them; stickler for playing by the rules; the mechanics of the game he called them. *They wouldn't write the damn things if you then make up your own!* He often said that if he'd had a frustrating evening."

"Often you say. Was he angry when he said this or merely frustrated?"

"He often laughed as he said it, Detective Chief Inspector. He also liked to spend time at those escape rooms."

Cyril raised his hand. "Escape rooms?"

"Yes, they are relatively new but you're put in a room, it's really like a stage set and you have to use clues to solve problems to find your way out. They're themed from what I understand. The doors are sometimes concealed or there's a combination locked gate. In some games you have to find an antidote as you have been infected. Sounds ridiculous, I know, but businesses use them for team building. He mentioned that once he was in a dungeon where there was only one barred exit visible; through solving a series of the clues, he got the numbers required to open the combination lock. You're given a set time to escape, usually an hour. He wanted us all to go. Can you imagine an undertaker's staff trying to escape from some kind of Egyptian tomb? Wouldn't be good for the business or our credibility if the press got to hear about it."

Owen chipped in. "I've heard of them. They're springing up in large towns. Newcastle has one. Ideal locations are old mills and buildings. The rooms are very well designed." He was looking at the Internet search on his phone. "*Lost, Cross-contamination, The Vacuum...* these are all scenarios with a description. You have sixty minutes." He passed the phone to Cyril so that he could look through the images.

"Do you know which he attended and if he went alone?"

"I think there's a minimum and maximum number for each booking."

"Did he ever mention friends by name, a girlfriend perhaps?"

"Boyfriends, yes but I doubt ever a girlfriend, not in that sense. He had female friends who played the games, I'm certain of that. Usually only referred to them by their Christian name. I recall a Fred, Martin, Karl, Spot, a nickname I assume. I can ask around. They'll be in his phone and believe me he always had that with him. Probably played games on it too." Duffers raise an eyebrow. "His phone is where to look, Chief Inspector."

"Owen!"

Owen understood and immediately left the room to call Control. They could check more quickly those businesses in the north east and run Carruthers's name. He also wanted them to run any names when his phone records came through.

"Did you know why Kevin might have recently withdrawn a large sum of money?"

Duffers answered immediately. "To do with payment for something to do with the new flat, I believe, extras. He told me he had enough to pay for extras so as not to load his mortgage. However, I couldn't be fully certain. Depends on what you call large Detective Chief Inspector."

Cyril nodded. "Thank you, right, that's useful to know. One last thing." Cyril always liked asking a question before leaving and he often allowed a pause after opening the sentence. "How did Kevin get to work daily? We know he didn't drive."

There was surprise that could be considered relief on hearing the question. "A sore point that, Detective Chief Inspector, a sore point. Failed his driving test at least four times. I kept saying that God was telling him something and that maybe he should give up. The problem was, Detective Chief Inspector, he didn't know his left from his right. He could never follow directions. Used to write on his hand so that he'd know. Doesn't work well when driving in traffic." He shook his head and smiled.

"So how did he get to work was the question?"

"He knew the route. Done it many times."

"Mode of transport, Mr Duffers?"

"Yes, sorry. He cycled most days unless the weather was really bad, then he'd catch a bus. It's not that far and he always changed out of his Lycra when he arrived. Showered and dressed in his more formal attire which was kept here. We make sure it's laundered. It's about standards."

There was a pause as Cyril pulled at his bottom lip. "We've just looked over his apartment but there was no bicycle."

Duffers laughed. "Some of the apartments in the three blocks have an external store, and one or two have garages. Kevin showed me the plans of the build and asked if I thought it worth having one. Now if you've ever lived in a flat you know the one thing you never have enough of is storage space. He pushed the boat out and bought a garage, that was one of the extras, the main one actually but in my opinion well worth the investment. He has three bikes and he stores his gear in there too. We went down to look when he moved in, a kind of house warming."

"Many there?"

"Yes, it was busy by the time I was leaving. There was Prosecco everywhere, bottle after bottle. Showed me the whole place. Really nice, great views from the back looking into the valley."

***

The journey back from Richmond was uneventful and Cyril survived relatively unscathed mainly due to Owen taking the A1M. The hour also gave him time to think. He would have loved to make notes but putting his head down and writing would have been an instant recipe to vomit. However, he did add a voice memo to his phone to check Carruthers's garage. Just as they were heading into Ripon Cyril received another call. Owen glanced sideways.

"It's April."

"Bennett."

"The victim is a John Van de Meer, thirty-one and lives in Howden." She did not make the mistake of giving him a geography lesson. "Same damage inflicted to the throat as the previous victim but I'm assured he still has both his hands. However, he doesn't have his ears. Both removed. As with the last case there doesn't seem to have been a disturbance, nobody heard anything out of the ordinary. The people in the next room heard movement and the toilet flush about one in the morning but that was it."

There was a pause as Cyril digested what he had just heard. "Confirm you said *ears*."

"Ears, sir, both. There's a difference in the amputation. According to this report the lobule on the right is still in place and the top twenty per cent of the left auricle is still present suggesting a rushed job."

Cyril tried to assimilate the information and visualise the damage. "CCTV?"

"There is in the entrance but someone has sprayed some kind of paint or grease on it. I've seen the clip. All you can see is a hooded figure, and then the hand holding a can before the spray hit the camera. After that, nothing."

"Property damage? Key system? So, no damage to any of the doors or windows? I take it they didn't have card keys just the old-style key in the lock?"

"Correct." April had not liked the way the investigation had developed all morning; it had all the hallmarks of retribution, someone was cancelling a debt in the most gruesome way. It had obviously been carefully planned and executed and in her opinion, whoever was carrying out these acts had been trusted or the victims had in some way been incapacitated. Either way, there was little chance of knowing if others were to follow with another full day of the convention left to run.

"April, I want all the details. Interview everyone still in the place. I also want the names and contact details going back twelve months of anyone who stayed in the deceased's room. Get someone to do the same for *The Grey House* as that's something we failed to do. I want as much information as possible back at the station as soon as."

***

After a further twenty minutes they were approaching Harrogate town centre.

"Castle Grey Skull looms into view," mumbled Owen, deepening his voice as if attempting to sound sinister. They turned off Otley Road and onto Beckwith Head Road.

"It's too modern, Owen."

"Not at dusk when the evening light falls on the stonework. Only needs turrets and there's enough weirdoes working in it... Present company excepted, of course."

Cyril glanced sideways as he placed the e-cigarette between his lips; soon a stream of vapour began to roll from his nostrils.

The dragon returns, Owen thought to himself as the car moved beneath the red and white security barrier.

Chapter Nine

Valerie Thew had just turned the key in the lock of the charity shop when the hand touched her shoulder. She instinctively jumped letting out a not too lady-like expletive.

"Sorry I didn't mean to startle you, Valerie. Sorry. Have you had an early lunch?"

She held her hands across her chest, her beige handbag on the crook of her left arm, the keys in her right hand. "Well if you didn't, I'd hate to experience it when you did, Jim West. Goodness, you nearly gave me a heart attack."

"I was just passing and I thought I'd pop in and say hello. I also wanted to let you know how much I enjoyed your company the other evening."

Valerie felt herself relax and her heart fluttered slightly. "Me too."

"I can't ask you out this evening as I play Mahjong tonight with a group from the U3A unless you want to come along and learn?"

She laughed. "Takes me all my time to play rummy. Far too complicated for me. Maybe another night."

"That would be lovely, yes." Jim smiled. "I'll call you." He turned and walked away from the shop.

Valerie returned his smile and waved. *That would be just what the doctor ordered, Jim West. Just what the doctor ordered.*

***

Owen brought a cup and saucer and placed it on the desk in the incident room. He held onto his mug.

"No hand and now no ears. You realise, sir, that if the first person had lost their eyes we could assume the missing ears meant hearing so if there's another body with a missing tongue, there'd be a connection as in the three wise monkeys…"

"But they didn't, Owen, did they? They lost a hand."

Owen pondered what he had said for a moment and then turned to Cyril. "Just thought."

"You know what thought did don't you?"

"Dustcart and wedding, sir." Owen raised his shoulders.

Something had been worrying Cyril since leaving the undertaker's and Owen's waffle did not help. "What do you make of these escape rooms?"

Owen sipped his tea; a drip from the bottom of the mug fell but missed both his clothing and Cyril's desk. "They're getting very popular, been around for a few years but it's not taken off like laser, paintball or bowling. It probably stemmed from things like *The Crystal Maze* programmes on TV."

Cyril raised his eyebrows. "*The Crystal Maze*? A crystal maze is a contradiction as you can see through the walls and therefore it would cease to be a maze… Pointless."

"That's on television too, sir. Are you sure you don't have a secret set?"

"Idiot's lantern, Owen." Cyril's voice was raised as his frustration grew. "I'll tell you about televisions and these new phones and tablets. Even when televisions were large and expensive boxes they used to sit in the corner of a room and stifle family interaction and now they're in every room. Families don't even sit together, kids upstairs, father watching football and the mother catching up on the soaps. Go into restaurants and nobody talks; they sit there looking at the illuminated lantern. In some ways, Kevin Carruthers had the right idea, as did those attending the convention. It's about talking and laughing together. Interaction, Owen, that's what real life's about, not this virtual bloody world that is meaningless and insincere."

There was a pause before Owen mumbled something about death.

"Pardon? Speak up, man."

"Bit dangerous if you ask me, this gaming business, from where I'm standing that is. We have two deaths, two murders involving two socially interactive human beings. If they'd stayed at home and watched telly they might still be alive today. Any road, going back to *The Crystal Maze*, it was on the TV. It's still on *You Tube*."

It was Cyril's turn to look confused.

Owen rested his mug on the desk before moving to the keyboard, bringing up *You Tube* on the large wall-mounted screen. "Now, sir, sit back and be educated in the power of the Internet." Harry Nixon came in as *The Crystal Maze* started to play. He pulled up a chair. "You'll see they take games to another level. Teamwork yet you play games as an individual. Interestingly, you can, if you have no confidence in one of your team, leave them locked up. Obviously on the telly show that's only make believe but... If you were a warped bugger you could cause mischief. Can you imagine setting one up in some semi-derelict mill and offering challenges, private challenges?"

"You could make enemies too if you were playing for high stakes," Harry added.

It was not lost on Cyril as he watched as the contestants each were given their set challenge, cheered on by the others who were outside the games room looking in and offering words of encouragement and on occasion clear advice.

Cyril frowned but could see the deviant direction in which Owen's imagination was taking him. "Immediate lock-in when too many mistakes are made, when the individual fails thereby putting pressure on the others in the team. That could make enemies of friends. I see what you're suggesting, Owen."

"My brother and two sisters used to come to blows over Monopoly," Harry chipped in, "especially at Christmas. It was like World War bloody three in our house."

"Simply sibling rivalry, Harry. Speaking of siblings, what of Carruthers's brother?"

Harry immediately responded. "Richard Carruthers. He's been notified and to be honest from all accounts he says that they didn't really get on after their mother passed away. Dispute over the mother's will apparently. Father had died twelve months prior. He has a clear alibi for the time running up to and of the murder. He's happy to come over if it will help but needs notice owing to work commitments."

"So, this we have seen is an escape room?" Cyril sipped the last of his tea.

"Similar in some ways but nothing like in another." It was again Harry who answered. "Owen asked me to check the games played but I noted that there was talk of escape rooms and so not knowing anything about them I did some digging; it's fascinating to be honest. There are businesses dotted around the country, usually big towns, that offer these as recreational games but also as team building exercises for businesses. Often they're very cleverly designed. Some I've seen are really extremely clever. They're all against the clock." Harry looked at Cyril.

"Awaiting April's feedback. Go ahead."

"Unlike that you have just witnessed now, these are organised differently. Still team building but the group of people work through the rooms together trying to collect something and then escape before the time is up. Nobody is at anytime isolated. So, let me give you one scenario I've seen. First you go through into what is a lift, an elevator. You have to work out where the new door is. Sometimes they're not as you would imagine and it may be a small passageway set behind some kind of panelling. Once in the next room you have to solve visual, skilful and technical clues in order to locate the object and then find the way out. Owing to the light quality it's not easy. Sometimes they have that dry ice giving a smoky atmosphere; helps hide the clues too. So, for example, there was a cave, an Egyptian tomb, a storeroom containing packing cases and even a laboratory where you had to find the magic tablets, the antidote you have to collect as you have been infected with a deadly virus that would kill you after sixty minutes. Each escape game company has different scenarios and they develop new ones on a regular basis to attract the gamers back."

"Carruthers was a regular user according to Duffers. He briefly described them too. Thanks, Harry. Get in touch with any escape rooms in the north east initially, make general enquiries, usual stuff, check if he booked in, if so with whom etc. Also see if they keep CCTV of the venue and also the rooms. I would imagine there's tight monitoring as far as Health and Safety is concerned."

"There's one here in Harrogate, just started up this year."

"Worth checking to see if either of the victims booked."

"I've checked… Nothing," Harry answered as he left. Owen followed.

***

Cyril checked his watch and his diary. He had to meet Dr Julie Pritchett, the pathologist, within the hour.

Chapter Ten

Cyril was always fascinated by Julie's office although he despaired at the layer of dust that seemed to be constantly present on the glass-topped surfaces. However, he also noted the initials he had drawn in the dust on his last visit were no longer present.

It was the jars and objects that always brought out his curious nature. He always avoided the pickled penis and he was not too enamoured by the tapeworm. To think something of that length could live inside the human body was just staggering. It reminded him of Owen's mention of the royal *we*. He glanced along the shelf at the many jars. It brought to mind the work by the artist Damien Hirst. There were no sharks, cows or sheep here but these jars held more of a conundrum. The wet specimen he studied looked like layers of bark, beige in colour but as he moved closer it appeared more like compressed tubing. He moved his hand towards the jar.

"Don't you dare, Bennett. Is nothing sacred? Rooting through a woman's personal private bits and pieces."

Cyril turned, a wide grin on his face. "Spoil sport!"

Julie had been watching him from the open door; she delighted in his morbid curiosity. "So I can only take your first answer, Cyril Vaughan Bennett, and if you fail you buy dinner. You know the rules, you've played the game before. But no touching."

He sat back down but his eyes never left the jar. "I'd say it's either the large or small intestine and if I have to choose it's going to be..." he paused looking towards Julie. "Large?"

"Asking or telling, detective?"

"Large... Telling." He raised his eyebrows and pulled a face that really showed he was not all that certain.

"Correct, Sherlock, so my turn to buy. Tonight, mind. I fancy Asian, the one opposite the Mercer, what's its name?"

"The Orchid." Cyril smiled. "Perfect. Now what do you have for me?"

Julie and Cyril had been in a relationship for some time but as they were both married to their professions, neither had wanted to take it further. Living separately suited their need for independence and so the status quo had been right for them both until now, but if the truth were known, Cyril had seen Julie in a different light upon the death of his father. Her sensitive understanding and support during his traumatic soul-searching had enabled him to make the correct decisions, clearing the fog of time and the anger of his youth; opening his eyes and allowing his feelings to flood out, for him an alien experience that once he would have considered a weakness. This caring support had brought a reunion with and appreciation of his stepmother, Wendy, after many years of false resentment. Suddenly, he had found this new relationship to be a blessing. He also knew that without Julie he would have lost this valuable and now precious part of his life. She had in fact helped him to find compassion, helped him to bury the hatchet.

***

April Richmond had finished collating the interviews taken from the residents of the *Victorian Guest House* and ensured that they would be added to HOLMES as well as updating the incident room boards. She had pulled up a chair and set about comparing the details from both cases. The similarities or coincidences were staggering and because of their exactitude she was of the belief that both murders had been planned and committed by the same person.

"Both in bed and breakfast establishments, both attending the games convention and from what we know to date, neither had met." She jotted down her thoughts in her notepad. "Both appear to have been killed in the same way from the looks of it although we'll know more when the post-mortem results are in. Both had a part of their anatomy removed posthumously."

"You can't talk to a better person, April." Shakti moved towards her resting a hand on her shoulder.

"Just thinking out loud, Shak. These deaths are so specific."

"Most serial killers' victims are. They follow a pattern, tend to be the same types. Look at the Yorkshire Ripper."

"They were just easy targets. If you arrive at particular areas in certain cities you can find them, Christ, they even climb into your car. These killings are different, they're more revenge, more payback. To me, they knew the killer, and in some ways trusted him. It appears as if it's some kind of end game."

"Have we checked this man's bank details? Remember Carruthers's was cleared out just before he died even though it all appears above board."

"In hand but at this stage everything seems in order."

"Have we had the toxicology results on Carruthers through yet?"

"Good point, Shak. I can't recall." She stood and moved closer to the boards allowing her finger to touch certain notes.

Shakti moved to the computer. "It's here." Both women crowded the screen and read in silence before turning to look at each other.

"That tells us a lot. Has Bennett seen this?"

***

Dr Julie Pritchett removed some photographs from a paper file and spread them out on her desk. "We managed to open the hand found in the park. As you're aware it had been shaped into a fist but it had been locked in position using Superglue. It wasn't late rigor mortis. Rigor mortis takes place when the body becomes totally stiff which can only last, as I'm sure you know, Cyril, twelve to twenty-four hours owing to the lack of adenosine triphosphate... ATP." She could see Cyril's eyes begin to glaze. "Sorry, after twenty-four hours, the stiffness dissipates and so to prevent that and to keep the hand locked as a fist it had been glued into position."

"So even an amputated limb goes through the same stages of rigor mortis as the rest of the body?"

"Give or take. Remember there are external factors that influence these changes but the times given are only rough guides."

Cyril looked at the photographs. "Does that spell the word, DICK?" he asked looking up at Julie.

"It appears to be written in ballpoint pen. Each letter is marked on the proximal phalanx of each finger. It's only written faintly and there's a good deal of skin damage resulting from separating the closed hand. As a matter of interest, Cyril, because the Superglue applied within the closed hand was difficult to remove, initially acetone was used but that can quickly defat the tissue. We decided to soak it. Alternatively, we could have left the hand untouched and in a day or so it would have been easier to open but we were unsure as to what the hand held even though it had been x-rayed. We were told speed was of the essence. So, if it does spell the word, *dick*, to be honest, I can't be sure of that, as those who have seen it have thought differently. If it wasn't written by Carruthers does a word written by another person offer any clues? Whoever glued the hand may well have been trying to protect that so it would be seen."

"Interestingly, according to his boss, Carruthers found distinguishing between his right and left hands difficult and would often write on one hand to differentiate." Cyril popped his glasses down his nose and looked again at the photograph. "He has a brother called Richard. As Eric Morecambe said, *Everyone knows you as Richard but you'll always be a Dick to me, son*." Cyril kept a straight face and then winked causing Julie to burst out laughing.

"Cyril Bennett, you're incorrigible."

"That would be too obvious anyway. Besides, we don't know if that's what it reads, it's a guess. If the killer did write it then it's a clue but as you have pointed out, it could even have been written by Carruthers and be part of one of the games he played in the days he was at the convention, or to know his right from his left. Had it been washed at all before he was killed?"

Julie, a little embarrassed, just shrugged as she had not considered that possibility owing to the processes used to remove the glue. What she did know was that the hand had been cleaned with some type of fluid after removal, probably to destroy any evidence, so that too could have had an effect on the ink. "From the initial tests we know it was bleached, cleaned... We'll do more checks. We've sent detailed photographs to a forensic writing expert. By the way, Carruthers could have written it as it's marked not on his dominant hand."

Cyril pulled a wry face suggesting it to be the more likely explanation. "Toxicology?"

"They've been received and forwarded. Thought that would be your first question on arrival. You obviously haven't seen them."

Cyril shook his head.

"One minute." She turned to the computer and brought the relevant file to the screen before swivelling it towards Cyril.

"So that suggests he was in some way drugged?"

"Eszopiclone is one of the more dangerous sleep-inducing drugs. It's from the class of drug known as sedative hypnotic, helps you sleep more quickly and keeps you in that state but it's also very addictive. We've checked with his GP and he's never been prescribed them; in fact it's four years since he last saw his GP so we can assume it was administered without his knowledge."

"No evidence of sex taking place?"

Julie shook her head. "There's no bruising other than to the area above the wrist where it was secured during amputation. There were no signs of a struggle."

"So was the amputation pre, or post mortem?" Cyril leaned forward a little uncertain, as the concept of bruising after someone had died confused him. Surely the blood would need to be pumping to cause a contusion.

"I'm sure I said, Cyril. Post."

"So, the bruising?"

"The bruising is known as pseudo bruising, indistinguishable to the eye from the type you would normally sustain. We see bruising occur during the post-mortem dissection procedures. It's to do with... Never mind."

Cyril frowned. "So how do you know that he wasn't held down before he was killed, held by the wrist, restrained before his throat was cut?"

Julie sat back and folded her arms as if separating herself from an audience. "Lesson one, sir. Bruising happens owing to the extravasion of blood. You know that?"

Cyril nodded.

"And this can occur close to the time of death where there is congestion of the cadaver and sufficient blood escapes post mortem to give the impression of bruising. However, this can lead to misconceptions. I used the term pseudo to denote the colouration around the amputation wound."

There was silence.

"We're on the same side, Cyril, remember?"

"Sorry!"

He pulled the photographs closer. "Considering where the hand was discovered and taking the glue into account, we can presume the killer wanted it found in that form. There must have been a reason."

"They wanted it found quickly as the glue would have deteriorated over a few days and the hand would have opened slightly."

"So as not to appear to be a fist?"

Julie nodded. "That might be significant."

"Is there anything else?"

"Just the splinter fragments beneath two nails, one with the corpse and one here..." She pushed a close-up photograph towards Cyril. "It's magnified so you can see it. What you can't notice are the traces of plaster of Paris."

"Clues?" Cyril looked apologetically at Julie knowing as soon as he had uttered the word that it was a foolish question. He raised a hand. "Sorry. It would be one of the first things you'd have told me."

Julie just smiled. "Hopefully they may get a result when we check his flat. I believe it was new, he hadn't been in long?" She watched Cyril nod. "Therefore, it could be from when he did some DIY. Are you aware that undertakers, or should I say morticians use plaster of Paris during some procedures?"

This really made Cyril sit up. "I didn't know that."

"Every day we learn." She slid her hand across the desk. "Pick me up at eight. No shop talk and I'll not mention what I did today."

Cyril withdrew his hand and he knew that he would have to wash it. Julie did too as she slid a bottle of hand gel across the table. "I don't want any excuses for a man-type illness. I remember your last bout of man flu."

They both laughed.

"Eight." Cyril left.

Chapter Eleven

S hakti repeated. "So *Flash* was unaware of these results?"
Cyril had received the sobriquet, *Flash,* not for the fact that he was always immaculately dressed but owing to his name. In the early days of his career, Cyril Bennett had carried the nickname, Gordon after an American playboy, Gordon Bennett, who enjoyed nothing more than to race cars and aircraft and collect beautiful women. The Gordon Bennett Tourist Trophy was awarded on the Isle of Man for one of their suicide races but it was for cars and not motorcycles. From Gordon came *Flash Gordon*, soon to be shortened to just *Flash*. Somehow it suited him.

April frowned. "Yes, he was when he left, but he's with the pathologist so I assume he'll have seen them by now. I'll request priority toxicology on John Van de Meer." April made the call before looking back at the boards.

"Van de Meer. What do we know?"

"As you see from the information boards, lives in a place called Howden; again, a single bloke. Moved back there in 2012. Teacher at a secondary school in Goole. Family have always lived in Howden. Parents were both teachers too. We've had a liaison officer there on and off since they were notified. They're in a dreadful state as you can imagine. According to the initial reports from…" she lifted a file. "… a DS Forsyth, John was a gamer and had played games all his life. Regularly went to these conventions especially during the school holidays, even ran a games club at school."

Shakti brought up Google Maps to see exactly where Howden was. "Bloody hell, looks like the back of beyond when you look at it here. Any friends?"

"Checking, but I did some research into these gaming conventions." April withdrew a sheet from her file. "They started in 2007 in the United Kingdom but they can be found worldwide and are more prolific than I first realised. Look at these figures for the years and attendees at one British location."

They both checked the statistics. "Bloody hell, April, that's some growth. In 2007 there were twelve hundred people attending and in 2018 just short of forty thousand."

"That's just one venue. It seems to me those who attend the same conventions also play locally and there's a strong camaraderie. It's the local meetings we have to find."

"Cyril has delegated that to Harry, I believe."

***

Harry Nixon had managed to borrow three of the games they knew Carruthers had played during his time at the convention and they remained on his desk. The rules, or the mechanics of the game as they were known to gamers, although not a huge tome, did seem increasingly complicated the more he read them. He had also made contact with a local gaming group who met on Tuesday evenings at the Fairfield Hotel between 7pm and 10pm. He had spoken to the organiser, a Mr West, and had arranged a meeting at the next games night. From the telephone conversation it seemed to him they were looking in the wrong place. Something nagged at him. Looking at the notice boards he checked for possible links. Clearly the way the victims had been murdered seemed identical, both occurring in a B&B with no sign of forced entry and they had attended the same venue the day before they were killed. It was as if they were murdered to a set of rules. The convention or the games played seemed irrelevant to him, there was something simpler and therefore decidedly more sinister. Why they were in Harrogate might well be totally irrelevant. Their accommodation and their room booking might well be the key to making inroads into the case. He would, however, know more after talking to Mr Jim West. He decided to call him again.

***

The balustrade looked just the same. Strange though how the condom had disappeared and yet the other items remained. There was no sight of the three objects previously thrown into the crushed stone.

"They've sunk into the ballast. Funny word… ballast… nautical term for stones used to stabilize a ship… Ballast." The words were said out loud but there was no one to hear them, drowned out by the drone of the traffic. "And the secateurs? Travelling the world and totally free."

A small beautifully painted figure was retrieved from a pocket along with a scalpel, the blade wrapped in a plastic sheath. The train was due any minute. Leaning over the stone ledge the instrument was held between finger and thumb. "And you too will leave this place to fall we know not where."

The sound of the train was suddenly audible and the vibration rippled the ground. Feet sensed the growing rumble as the sound increased; the train appeared from beneath the road like magic as it gained speed. As it passed, the knife was dropped, landing on the roof of the carriage. He raised a hand and waved at the passing train. However, the disposal of the object and the strange behaviour did not go unnoticed.

***

Cyril walked up Robert Street leaving ample time; the walk to Julie's apartment normally took about twenty minutes. He would have a drink with Julie first and the taxi should arrive by 8.30. He had planned that Julie would stay over at his house and they could walk back from the restaurant if the weather stayed fine. Approaching Granby Road, he paused and looked around, taking in the magnificence of The Stray. Very few towns had the luxury of two hundred acres of open grassland within the centre. Fortunately, it was well managed for the benefit of all. He took a deep breath. *The lungs of the town,* he said to himself as he continued his walk.

The gate was open as Cyril walked up to the door. He glanced at the bay window. The Venetian blinds were open, but on the tilt, making it difficult to see into the room. He rang the bell. He saw fingers part the slats and one finger appear. He was never sure if it would be one or two, either way it usually brought a smile. Not everyone was greeted by such an affectionate show. He heard the electronic lock *click* and he pushed the door open. The hallway was immaculate, the black and white marble tiles, the flower bedecked side-tables giving the space a homely feel.

"You're early." Julie's voice carried from the ground floor apartment and resonated in the space. "Drinks are poured."

"I was always told that when you walk into a pub and your drink appears on the bar without your asking it is time to find another pub."

"Firstly, for a policeman, your analogy is suspect for this is neither a pub, nor is your drink on a bar and secondly, DCI Cyril bloody Bennett, never look a gift horse in the mouth." She greeted him with a kiss before quickly wiping away the trace of lipstick she had transferred.

He saluted, picked up the two glasses and handed one to Julie. "May these be the worst of our days. Cheers!"

***

The 101 call came into control and it was logged and recorded at 17.34.

"I was waiting at the lights and I witnessed someone dropping something onto the passing train... strange thing was they then waved either at the train or at the object. Maybe it's something and nothing but for the sake of a call you just never know. Hope I'm not wasting anybody's time."

North Yorkshire police had invested heavily in their new control technology and since the introduction of the operator or callback services, the system worked more smoothly. After the brief call, Hussain Green felt comfortable he had done his civic duty. If they needed further information they would call him back.

The information was transferred to the British Transport Police. Within forty minutes a Railtrack vehicle was parked off the road in front of the bridge. One of the Trackmen moved down the banking after informing their control of an officer near or on the line. The procedure was straightforward. He scoured the lines first but could see nothing that might interfere with the next train. He then walked a short distance up either side of the tracks but apart from collecting part of a pram he saw nothing else.

"Can't have been this," he said holding up the object. "Looks as though it's been here ages." He tossed it into the grass at the side. Scrambling back up the banking he took one last glance but could see nothing. He called his control to say the line was clear.

***

Alan Bowen and David Hale walked up Parliament Street. Both were in their late twenties. They had met on a number of occasions since starting work at the same local supermarket. Both were single men. They tried to arrange one night out a week if their work commitments allowed. Alan lived in Pudsey near Leeds and David near Yeadon. Their friendship had developed from almost the first week of working together. Being of a similar age, they had the same sense of humour and both were into puzzles and pub quizzes. However, it was their love of escape rooms that had cemented their developing relationship. Over the months they had visited centres in Manchester, Leeds, Newcastle and tonight they were in Harrogate.

"So what time are we aiming for?" Alan glanced sideways tapping his pocket where he kept the notebook in which he recorded all his games. They turned onto Cambridge Road before crossing to James Street.

"I'll be disappointed if we take longer than fifty minutes. I've brought the best brain Pudsey has to offer."

The escape room challenge was set against the clock. The majority of centres had a time of sixty minutes and the rooms were graded according to the complexity of the puzzles and clues to find the way out. They always chose the most difficult scenario that could be played by two people.

"Will we ever escape?" David slapped him on the back. "Best brain... Jesus! Which escape game do you want to try?"

"CSI experience looks intriguing. You?"

"Those that allow only two players," he said sarcastically and received a slap at the back of the head. "Any. Just want to get on. I'm buzzing!"

***

Julie slipped her hand across the table. "How's your mum?"

Cyril lifted his eyes on hearing the word *mum*. He did not correct her.

He had not been in contact with his father for a number of years before his final days. An incident in his youth where he had witnessed him having an affair with his mother's best friend had brought with it an emotional turmoil made worse by the discovery of his mother's terminal illness. However, it was more complex than it had originally seemed as his mother had encouraged her friend, Wendy, to have the affair knowing Wendy had also always loved his father. She wanted to ensure on her passing that Cyril would continue to receive a mother's love. Things in life seldom go the way they are planned and his mother's best efforts failed to bring any unity until the day of his father's funeral. It was only then he saw the qualities in Wendy that his mother had recognised so long before.

"She's fine. I ring her every couple of days. Need to go over soon to sort out the Bentley if your dad can spare the time and he still wants to babysit."

Julie just nodded and smiled before squeezing his hand. "He's been so excited. He'll be a boy with a new toy. You must promise though, Cyril, to take me out in it at least once a year."

Cyril had been working up to this moment for some time, it had not been easy and he had shied away from it... somehow the time and the place had never seemed right but tonight, a favourite restaurant... it would be perfect. He was just slipping his hand into his pocket when Julie spoke again.

"I know I said no dead body or work talk but I need to chat briefly about Van de Meer. What have you found out about his past?"

Cyril immediately released the small package he had grasped in his pocket and withdrew his hand. His heart sank. It took him a moment to regain his composure. "Teacher, maths, comes from Hornby. No police record. Heavily into games, board type games not the computer variety."

"Partner?"

"As far as we know, no. Why?"

Cyril had taken the opportunity to take a drink, his mouth had suddenly become dry.

There was a brief pause. "He's not a man."

Having just sipped his pint of Black Sheep when she said it he choked briefly trying to keep what was left in his mouth from escaping. "He's what?"

"Female, Cyril. DSD. Disorder of Sexual Development. You don't want me to go through this here but the autopsy clearly shows that although he had the chromosomes of a man, the genitals are not fully formed and he has a uterus. It used to be called pseudohermaphroditis but we use another term today. Thought you should know but whether it has any relevance to the case, I can't say. I'm checking with his GP and his medical history. Have you traced the family members?"

"Yes. So he's a homosexual?"

"That doesn't necessarily follow nor apply but this is not…" She could see from Cyril's expression he was not really taking anything in.

Cyril was simply staring at the beer before turning his attention back to Julie. He could not believe what he was hearing. She kept eye contact but sipped her gin and tonic as if she had just passed comment on the weather.

"You're just full of surprises, Julie Pritchett. Must be why I love you so much." He paused running his finger around the rim of the glass, a little confused and feeling thrown way off course.

Julie watched him waiting for some obscure comment but she could only see his lips move; there was no sound.

"I've… sorry, a minute… I've been meaning to ask you this for some time but maybe after that bombshell this isn't the right time even though this place is perfect. It's been on my mind for a while…" He collected his thoughts, slipping his hand back into his pocket. His fingers found the small box.

Cyril had not noticed the waiter appear to his blind side. "Mr Bennett, sorry to intrude but your table is ready." He bent and collected the two drinks before popping them on a tray. "This way, please."

Cyril knew the moment was lost along with his appetite and left the box where it was.

Chapter Twelve

"**M**ay I speak to Mr Jim West, please?"
"Speaking."

Harry explained that although he still wanted to visit the group he needed to meet before that date just to help guide an investigation.

"I'm free this evening. Is it not possible to discuss it on the phone?"

"It will take less than an hour, sir."

Jim West agreed that they would meet in forty minutes.

***

Harry checked the address was correct and pressed the button for West's apartment. There was no answer. He tried again. On this occasion it was answered. A voice that seemed to be squeezed through the intercom appeared unnaturally high.

"Hello?"

"DC Nixon, Mr West. You're expecting me."

Harry heard the lock electronically open and pulling the door towards him he entered. He immediately smelled the lingering aroma of recently smoked marijuana and paused; it seemed to be coming from the bin store. The door was ajar and the light was on. To his right was a flight of stairs; there was no carpet and a distant sound of rap music echoed in the empty corridor. Harry climbed the stairs taking two steps at a time and quickly saw Jim West standing by his apartment door. A broad smile was the first welcoming experience he had received since his arrival. It did not last.

"Smelled it did you?" West asked defensively. "If I had a pound for every time I've reported the behaviour of some of the families in these apartments I wouldn't be living here. Sorry, come in. You're not here to listen to my moaning."

The room was immaculate and Harry let his eyes take in the orderly space, something most coppers did. Part of the walls was lined with display cabinets and all of the shelves were filled with hundreds of small figures each beautifully painted. Along the top sat a regimented line of model buildings, many deliberately made to resemble ruins, again painted in the most realistic way. He moved closer and looked through the glass doors.

"How many do you have?" Harry found himself trying to count those he could see on the upper shelf.

"I've lost count. It gets to you and painting them is as great a part of gaming as actually playing the games."

"Must have taken you hours," Harry said turning back to look in another cabinet.

"If only. Years, yes, and I have many more waiting to be painted. I order new games constantly, I'm addicted." He simply shrugged his shoulders.

"Are those Nazi figures?" Harry pointed to an area near the back.

"Zombi Nazis, they're part of a game. Very popular and the detail on those is amazing, works of art in reality." Jim opened the cabinet door and brought one out before handing it to Harry. "I try to paint wearing gloves but for the fine detail you don't have the feeling, hence this." He held out his hands and Harry could see the traces of paint beneath the fingernails on his right hand. There was a long silence.

Harry shook his head. "Those, dare I say, are absolutely fantastic. Bloody gruesome, but I'm impressed. Are these allowed with the swastika displayed so clearly?"

"Works of art? They are indeed. Those are made in America. I invest via a company called *Kickstarter.* Designers pitch their games and players like myself can invest, it means we get the games a lot cheaper if they achieve the funding required or we get our money back. It's not only games, it supports all kinds of entrepreneurial ventures." He paused briefly. "Come this way." He led Harry to another room. "It's addictive so hence the unpainted figures in all of these boxes. It's supposed to be the spare bedroom... my office. If you think I have lots here you really don't want to see what some gamers collect. I am, in their eyes at least, an amateur. Not for the painting, mine take some beating, but in quantity!"

Harry laughed. "I'll take your word for it, Mr West."

"May I offer you a drink?" Jim asked.

"No, thank you."

The conversation went on for longer than either had planned and when Harry looked at his watch it was going on for ten. He had found the meeting extremely valuable enabling him to consolidate his thinking.

"You've been most kind, Mr West." Harry turned to leave but then paused. "May I ask if you're now retired? I don't see with all of these how you could possibly find time to work."

"I am now. I used to have a small business just out of Harrogate town centre but times were getting difficult for independents. The Internet and buying online keeps people away. That's a story for another time. Before that it was the theatre. Are you still planning to come along on Tuesday? You'll then have a better understanding of what it's all about."

"I'll look forward to that, thank you. One last question." Harry turned and pointed to a large green model figure standing in splendid isolation.

Jim West laughed. "The figure of all figures in my opinion. *Cthulhu* is a fictional, cosmic entity born from the magical, imaginative mind of H P Lovecraft. It was created in 1928."

Harry raised his eyebrows. "Look it up when you've a minute." Jim scribbled the name on a piece of paper and handed it over.

"Sorry for the lingering aroma of illegal drugs in the passageway but if you know a friendly officer it would be appreciated."

"I'll have a word." Harry stuck out his hand. "Thank you very much, it's been most valuable."

"Gamers can be very dedicated and quite fanatical as you can see. We take great pride in the manner in which we play and the way we present our games. If I can help in any way don't hesitate…" He let the words drift into the hallway allowing the smell of cannabis to take their place. On closing the door he moved back to the green figure and lifted it with a degree of reverence. "They come sniffing about but…"

***

Alan Bowen and David Hale were comfortable in each other's company and were set for the challenge. Alan checked his watch; they were early. The room was booked from 7.30. They had a coffee and waited, discussing what tactics they might require to beat the time. Each was becoming increasingly more excited as they approached the venue.

They had decided to play the escape room based around the Pharaoh's tomb and it had been more complicated than either had initially imagined even though it was graded four-star difficulty. They had not expected such poor lighting and some of the clues had been concealed under the fairly thick layer of sand that covered the floor. At 8.11 David located the small, faience-like ushabti figure and held it up triumphantly. They could now make progress and look for the way out.

"Any clue on the figure?" Alan asked reverently holding the blue figurine to the nearest light source. He let the light illuminate the turquoise blue of the plastic figure.

"Four letters but they're difficult to make out. Give me a moment. Could say *Fake* but it might be nothing."

Alan came over and lifted his glasses as if it would help him to discern the letters. *"Take.* Look the figure has no left hand, lost at the wrist, so take left or right-hand wall?" He looked at his partner, a huge grin appearing. "We have time. Left or right?"

David moved to the right-hand side of the sarcophagus that was positioned in the centre of the tomb. Various artificial stone blocks were stacked on either side. He then noticed that two had lids held closed with a combination lock comprising four tumblers.

"The numbers must be on the side." Each man searched the hieroglyphs that were decorating the sarcophagus.

"4… 7… 9… 4." Alan called out as David fumbled with the tumbler.

"It's open!"

Inside the box was a sheet of papyrus giving the final clue. Within minutes they were out. The clock had stopped at fifty-one minutes. Each man shook hands and congratulated the other.

"That was more difficult than I'd originally thought. Should be a five-star escape."

After handing the figure in and receiving a small certificate recording their time they left. A beer was definitely in order.

"*Coach and Horses*?" David did not need asking twice. He checked the time. "Train isn't for another hour, we might manage a couple."

***

On leaving the venue, the two men were so relieved at beating the time, they had taken little notice of their surroundings. Although not fully dark, the streetlights and the shop window displays cast coloured light onto the road. The way was easy to follow, both were excited and their laughter seemed to echo around the buildings.

He simply followed cautiously, occasionally stopping to look in shop windows to ensure the gap between them remained constant. Seeing them turn into the pub he waited a moment, glancing at the skeleton riding the penny-farthing cycle that hung on the outside wall of the building.

The *Coach and Horses* was busy but then it always was. The two men were standing by the bar.

"Excuse me."

Alan and David turned and noticed the man waiting to get to the bar and they moved to one side creating room. "Sorry."

He smiled. "Thanks. Did you succeed?"

David turned to look at the man. "Succeed?"

"As I was coming here I noticed that you two came out of the escape rooms. Great fun. It's not been here long, couple of months maybe. Had me beaten the first time I went in. Totally bamboozled." He turned away and ordered a beer.

The atmosphere changed immediately and both David and Alan turned and introduced themselves. The man nodded saying nothing in return but he quickly took a blue figure from his pocket. He handed it to the nearer man.

"Bloody hell, the ushabti figure! That was our lifeline. Without finding that we'd have been buggered." He looked at the back of the small figurine and read what was on the back... *take*. "Fifty-fifty chance of getting it right in the time we had, it was an important call," Alan laughed.

"Or wrong," said their new friend. "All chance. I got it wrong and ran right out of time. I thought it would be where the hand was missing... story of my life. I blamed the guy I was with mind."

"How come you've got the figure?"

"Consolation prize, I guess. You keep it, you deserve it more than I do."

Both men looked at each other. "The victor's trophy," Alan said holding it aloft. "Let me buy you a drink in return."

"No, I'm expected home." He drank the remains of his glass and turned to go. "I have a friend who's creating his own experience in the hope of making it a business. It will be here in Harrogate and he's looking for enthusiasts to try out the games he has designed. If you're interested I could pass him your contact details. He says that they'll be no push over, unlike many around the country. Up to you."

Alan and David looked at each other and then at the figure. Alan picked up a beer mat from the bar and jotted down their names and his mobile number.

"It'll cost him a pint if we escape," David suggested.

The man smiled, tapped the beer mat and shook their hands. "He'll be in touch. It might cost you more if you lose."

They simply laughed. "Two pints?"

Nothing else was said.

Watching him leave David looked at the figure.

"What do you think?"

"Let's wait and see. If he calls we'll think about it then."

Chapter Thirteen

The sky augured rain. Large clouds seemed to hang in billowing bags threatening to burst and spill their contents at any time. DC Rodcliff Massiah pressed the remote for the garage door as two CSI officers readied themselves. He had already dressed in the appropriate disposable clothing so as not to compromise the scene. He was unsure what to expect other than the three bikes, probably bits of decorating equipment and some packing cases. According to the brief it would be simple and routine.

Rodcliff Massiah had been born in London. His parents, both natives of the parish of St James, Barbados, had moved to England and the city the year he was born. Always diligent at school and conscious he was an only child, he knew his parents had always expected the best from him. The early years had not been easy for his parents and he felt a real weight of responsibility. He had always had a dream of becoming a police officer. He had heard stories from his own grandfather who had attained the rank of Inspector in the Barbados Police Force, spending most of that role stationed at Holetown Police Station. Seeing his grandfather in uniform and being shown round the station were the catalysts for his wanting to join the force. After five years in three different roles in The Met he had transferred to plain clothes and moved to Northallerton.

Policing the capital had been a challenge that filled his expectations but he was eager to see his career develop. Colleagues had warned him the move *up north* would in fact prove to be a retrograde step but he thought differently. To him, opportunities were what you made of them. Enthusiasm and dedication would always be appreciated and noted. On his leaving, a close friend had given him a gift and on the card she had written, *Never let the doubters win, Rodcliff!* It had become his mantra and so far, he had proved them wrong.

He and the attending CSI had been called back to Carruthers's flat after receiving the information regarding the garage. He watched as the door slowly rose and on this occasion was allowed to go up to its limit. There was a slight flutter in his stomach as he remembered they were part of a murder investigation. He could see the bikes and the rack of clothes lit by the single LED light that had automatically illuminated as the door was activated, but within minutes it had dimmed.

The CSI moved forward lighting the area with strong free-standing battery lamps, but these would soon be augmented by the garage lights themselves once the switch had been dusted for prints. Within fifteen minutes they had worked through the first section of the garage. Tread mats had been placed leading up to the inner door which was left ajar. Massiah was looking into an inner room whilst awaiting permission to enter and he was amazed by what he saw as the two CSI started their work.

"Looking at this lot we could be here for some time. And to be honest I have a strange feeling about this place." Her gloved hand pointed to the row of skulls positioned along the shelf as she slipped her mask below her chin.

Massiah nodded his head inadvertently as he counted twenty-two skulls all equally spaced and yet all of differing sizes.

"They're not real," the CSI chuckled, "but what a strange bloody thing to find, particularly knowing the owner was an undertaker."

"Brought his work home with him that's all... don't we all," retorted the other sarcastically. "Come in but tread careful..." He did not finish. "Oh you beauty. We have a camera here poking out from behind this one." He traced the lead to the socket on the wall. "Looks to be a sound and motion jobby. Probably records brief clips when triggered by either movement or sound. Stored on an internal mini disc I imagine. We'll secure that and process as soon as."

Massiah simply watched as they photographed the camera, marking its position before bagging it. They had been photographing and sampling for about fifty minutes when they noticed something.

"Look in each cabinet and tell me what you see," one of the CSI said, her voice challenging the detective to match her observations.

He took a moment to study each cabinet and then he retraced his steps without taking his eyes off the challenge. His hand moved to the glass on the second one. "There's a figure missing," he said, a little uncertainly. He looked again.

"Out of all these, and we're talking bloody hundreds, there's one missing. You can see where it sat from the lack of dust."

"And there are no others?"

"Nothing else. Why that one? And what figure was it?"

"Looking at the dust mark it's clearly larger than the rest. Anyone who's as meticulous as this may well have photographs of each cabinet and if so, let's hope they're either somewhere in here, on his phone or in *the cloud.*"

"Maybe on camera?" Massiah said hoping he was not stating the bleeding obvious.

"Or on the camera," came back the reply.

***

Harry knocked on Cyril's office door. "A minute, sir?"

"Come in, Harry. All okay?"

"I need to run something past you."

Cyril pointed to the chair.

"Called on Jim West last night, the guy who's into games. Immaculate flat but bloody hell, sir, these people take their passion for this kind of thing to a different level."

Cyril just sat back before adjusting his tie.

"It's not just games as we know them but ones using a shed full of figures, zombies… even Nazi zombies sporting swastika emblems. I thought that was illegal but he assures me that they are popular the world over. Anyway they paint them and keep them in display cabinets. That's what takes their time, painting the things."

"Do they use them?"

"Yes, and they're proud of them too."

Cyril made a note to check the Nazi legality before also noting the word zombie in block capitals and the word *Caribbean* after it.

"Anyway, they buy into ideas for new games using a website and this is mutually beneficial helping the designer and the gamer as they get the new games at a reduced rate."

This information did not appear to be exciting his boss. He could see him bouncing his pencil on his lower lip and so he waited.

"Rodcliff Massiah." He looked at Harry.

"Come again, sir."

"We have a DC Rodcliff Massiah working with the CSI people at Carruthers's garage and we've received these initial reports and images." Cyril swung the computer screen around.

"That's bloody spooky. That's just like West's place but he doesn't have all those skulls and the gothic-like chairs. West's isn't painted black either… that's as dark as the bloody grave if you ask me."

"It certainly was as neat as a grave. For a bloke, it was immaculate. Apparently, the place was perfect apart from one missing piece, some type of figure it's believed, taken from one of the cabinets. We're checking a simple camera found behind one of the skulls. When we get the footage we might have an answer. I want Massiah to pop down to Harrogate. I need to chat with him about the garage. Please arrange it, Harry. And Harry, find out all you can about zombies."

"Escape rooms, games and now zombies. To think I used to nick folk for speeding. How times have changed."

Just as he was about to leave, the reason he had come to see Cyril in the first place came back to him. "Might be something and nothing but the deeper I'm looking into this the more concerned I am that we're doing just that, we're looking too deeply… zombies! For Christ sake! What if the deaths have nothing to do with games or the convention or Harrogate even? What if they're all to do with the hotel and the specific rooms where the murders took place? The similarities there are credible."

"Bring your ideas to the briefing tomorrow morning. All ideas can be good ideas, Harry."

"Did you get any further info about Van de Meer's medical condition? Did it affect his family or personal relationships?"

"We should know more tomorrow when all the findings will be discussed at the briefing."

***

Jim West checked his watch before crossing Parliament Street in front of Betty's Tea Room. He neither heard the crossing's constant beeping nor saw the flashing man, he simply focused on his thoughts. He walked briskly past the Cenotaph and down Cambridge Street; since becoming pedestrianised, the area was usually busy with shoppers and the occasional busker. Jim smiled to himself as he recalled Harrogate's famous busker, Rudy, the Jamaican, who often stood wrapped in a duffle coat and who sang the words of Bob Marley so enthusiastically. Jim paused at the spot where Rudy would often sing bringing a hint of the Caribbean to the wet and wintery Harrogate street. This spot was his world stage and how welcome he had been. However, within an instant, Jim's mood changed at the sight of a young man huddled near the same spot simply sitting with a paper cup in front of him ready to take, but appearing to have nothing to give. "How times change," he mumbled to himself.

Checking his watch again he realised that he was early. He had hoped to see Valerie but he had forgotten it was her day off. However, it was of little consequence, he had much to do.

***

Cyril watched the section of captured footage taken from the camera set in Carruthers's garage. It recorded the date and the time and considering the quality of the equipment the images were remarkably clear.

Carruthers could be seen checking the garage before bending away from the lens and although the sound was evidence that he was still moving, his hands were out of shot. After a few seconds, however, he was back in view. "Bingo!" Cyril quickly paused the shot. It was there in his hand, the object that was missing from the cabinet. He restarted the film and watched as the figure came to his lips and he saw him kiss it. The sound too was clear.

"We shall work together, and we shall be the victors."

Cyril paused and rewound to hear the words again. "We shall work together, and we shall be the victors."

He started it again and watched as Carruthers popped the figure into a soft bag.

"We shall," Cyril said slowly, "and not we will work or we will be victors?" The formality of the language confused him. Looking again at the screen he focused on the figure in Carruthers's hand. He enlarged the shot before reaching for the phone and dialling an internal extension. Harry Nixon answered.

"Harry, just look at the footage from Carruthers's camera. Two things come to mind. It's clear what his most prized possessions were. He didn't have a camera in the apartment but he did in the garage but not where you'd think… it wasn't positioned where the most valuable items were stored. I'm assured the cycles were worth a good deal of money. Secondly, it shows him kissing what is believed to be the only missing figure from the cabinets. What do you know about it?"

"Give me five minutes."

The two men looked at the printed images Cyril had produced from the screen and set them next to the report from Massiah and the forensic results.

"The place is more like an inner sanctum, a shrine to the games. The full results aren't in as one or two of the games and a selection of what appear to be the most used figures are being checked for prints and DNA. He didn't play on his own in there. There's no one else on the camera disc history other than Carruthers who appears always to enter alone before turning the camera off. We then see him switch it back on. If you check, the chairs show that they have been moved during that period, so we can presume others were in the room. That though is not a crime. What do you know of that figure? Looking at the photographs of the cabinets, Harry, I can see many that appear to be identical or at least similar, let's say more of a human form. But that one?"

"That one's very special, it's Cthulhu, created by a guy in the 20s. The story featuring the figure was published within pulp fiction. It's a gigantic entity worshipped by cultists. Others have extended the mythology and tried to link it with Satanism... there's even a Cthulhu bible created around it. Some also believe it to have racist overtones."

"Racism?" Cyril frowned. "There's little evidence to date but we'll note that. However, Satanism? So, what about the skulls? Linked in some way to his profession? Where's this leading?" Cyril did not give time for responses, it was like a verbal thought process.

"In my opinion, sir, it's leading nowhere to be honest. We're seeing all of this paraphernalia and are reading too much into it. Let's look at it from a different perspective. Let's imagine if we'd believed Carruthers to be a killer and we'd stumbled on this lot then... it would make some kind of sense but he was the first victim. Let's wait until we get the full forensic results back."

"So, do you think this Cthulhu model could just be a good luck charm collected to take with him during his participation at the Harrogate Games Convention?"

"Simply that, yes."

Cyril agreed to wait. Caution regarding judgements was probably the best course of action at this stage.

Shakti appeared at the door. "Latest from forensics. DNA of both men found within the garage."

"On what?" Cyril knew he needed the DNA to be located on a static source.

"Found on a number of the figures and two games but also on the table."

"So he was in the room. They knew each other. What about the apartment?"

"Clear evidence Van de Meer was there, even if it were only to use the bathroom. However, you remember Duffers reported that there'd been a house warming. Who knows?"

"Thanks Shakti. Written up?"

"ASAP." She left as quickly as she had arrived.

Chapter Fourteen

The appearance of both amputated ears could best be described as resembling two seashells. Neither was now pink but had taken on a grey-brown tone not dissimilar to that of tanned flesh. The exposed area where they had been separated from the body was now darker, possibly best described as maroon, almost the colour of a bruise.

"Concha... concha, a perfect description. How like shells you look."

A gloved hand picked up the first and allowed it to rest on the palm. "No weight at all and still so flexible."

The hand closed folding the body part within its grasp. Most of the ear is cartilage combined with some muscle and therefore yields with ease. As the hand opened, the ear began to unfurl.

"Listening is one of man's greatest gifts... it's a real skill. Empathy... It's so true what they say, that wise words often fall on deaf ears. You're not listening now!"

On closer inspection, the scarring on the lobule showed evidence of past piercings in more than one place but it was obvious that an earring had not been inserted for some time. This would now change. Carefully, the small silver point punctured the healed wound before exiting the rear of the lobe. The retaining clip was firmly locked at the back tight against the dead skin. The ear was held at arm's length.

"That looks perfect."

He collected both ears and popped them into a transparent freezer bag before slipping it into a pocket. He needed one more piece of equipment and all would be ready.

**

The room was full as Cyril tapped his electronic cigarette against his now empty china cup. It rang with an expected clarity and the room fell silent.

"Morning everyone. Thank you for your time and attention."

A few greetings came back but they sounded more like groans.

"We've a good deal on our plate and a number of avenues we need to consider and place into some kind of perspective. You should all be up to speed if you've read the boards and the reports. The system has also thrown up a number of connections which require further analysis."

There was an immediate shuffling of paper from all areas of the room and faces turned to the boards.

"Shakti, you've been looking at Van de Meer's medical condition. What do we have?"

"Condition from birth and the parents decided from the outset that no medical intervention should take place. *What will be will be* was their attitude and after a degree of legal wrangling that is what happened. From our meetings with the parents it appears John showed all the traits of being a boy. Whether this was because of biased parenting we'll never know. No serious problems at school, the odd bullying but I guess that's normal and no reports of psychological issues. The pathologist has seen his medical records and there has been no medical intervention other than the standard childhood illnesses. What's clear from the research we've managed to conduct is that John Van de Meer kept himself to himself. We've learned from interviews with family members and neighbours he was academic and a loner, not many relationships and few real friends. The ones he did have were, other than those within the clubs where he played games, predominantly female. However, it's clear from this information he's only had a couple of what might be classed as steady girlfriends. No problems at work, well liked, good class discipline. Everything on the surface seemed fine."

"Post-mortem?"

"As with the first, clear evidence from toxicology that the same drug was administered resulting in a deep sleep. Owing to the quantity taken, Van de Meer was probably in a comatose state and therefore unable to defend himself. Like the first victim, the body parts were removed post mortem. Cuts to the neck are consistent with the first murder. Considering the similarity of the incisions, the depth, the angles and direction of cut, it's more than likely the injuries were carried out by the same person. You can also see in the report that the glass used is a perfect match for that used against victim one; similar minute fragments were found. The photographs showing the damage to the side of the head give a clear idea of the amount of the ear that was amputated. Note that neither is the same. It's apparent the person doing this was not concerned with removing all of the ear."

Cyril waved a finger. "Or deliberately performed the cutting this way for reasons only known to themselves. Surely with a scalpel and a corpse there was no need to rush things. I've seen ears removed in fights, bitten off and they look a little like that." He looked round the room hoping others would support his point of view but he seemed to be alone in his belief. "Any signs of sexual activity?"

"As in case one, no. No other injuries either."

April's phone signalled a message. She checked it, stood, went to the nearest computer and began typing. Cyril watched as Shakti continued with her report.

"Sir?" She paused distracted by April.

"Sorry, Shak. A minute."

Shakti nodded resting her notes on the table.

April continued to read as all eyes turned to her. "Forensics have found identical Low Copy Number DNA traces of a person unknown on the clothes of both victims. It's been run through the system but there's no reference; we don't hold that person's DNA identity on file."

There appeared to be a collective sigh of disappointment in the room. Shakti sat down instinctively.

"However, there is a positive match from that collected in both B&B rooms. There's also a suggestion that the samples taken there were from a different time period owing to where they were collected and the degradation." She pulled a face to suggest it was beyond her. "Can you believe that one match identified was taken from a small toenail clipping found in the corner of the bathroom at *The Grey House* and the second was a piece of dried nasal mucus discovered within the carpet at *Victorian Guest House.* I doubt anyone committing a murder would then break off to give themselves a pedicure."

Laughter brought a little light relief allowing Owen to add to it.

"The dear old bogey," announced Owen with a degree of relish. "Sticky, picky, rolly, flicky!" His grin said it all.

Cyril quickly broke in before any other person in the room who wanted to become a comedian could add their own joke.

"The bastard's been in those rooms before and a tenner says he took away the bloody keys." There was a sudden enthusiasm within each word. "He's a past bloody resident. Went off with the keys and either took a copy before returning them or didn't even bother to do that."

Brian Smirthwaite spoke for the first time. "He must have had a crystal ball, sir, if he knew his victims were going to be in the same room as him at some time in the future, or does it mean he or she just killed for the sake of it and they were indiscriminate victims who'd been given that room? Fate can be a bugger."

Cyril mused, "So it might have nothing to do with the convention, nothing to do with chance just to do with the single occupancy of those rooms."

"And if he did this in two venues what's to say he hasn't done it in more B&Bs and hotels and we're simply waiting for the next victim," suggested Brian.

"The rooms are both doubles. How did our killer know they were occupied by singles?"

Cyril scanned the room and it was clear from what he saw that this scenario could well have traction.

"By invitation?" a relatively new detective within the group whispered to a colleague sitting close by.

"Keys. Who was asking the owners about keys that had gone missing, taken by mistake and either been returned or not?"

An officer near the back of the room stood. "Quinn, sir. Harry instructed me to make enquiries. Neither did, I mean they didn't and still don't keep a record. It happens, the loss of keys, but not as frequently as to make an issue of it. They always keep spare keys, and in most cases, once the guest has realised the error the keys are usually returned. *The Grey House* once had keys returned from Russia."

"Thoughts please." Cyril tapped his pencil against his hand as he spoke. He was eager to pursue this new information.

"We know that the two deceased were acquainted with each other. DNA found at the garage bears that out. I take it we've checked with Van de Meer's parents to see if they have ever met or were acquainted with Carruthers? You just never know, all this might be a family issue. I take it we have alibis for his parents on the night of the murder?"

Owen leaned sideways. "Reports on the board, sir."

Cyril allowed it to pass and continued. "So on the night they died they were both close to the same person when they were clothed. Keeping an open mind that could have been during the convention or even when walking back to their digs. There was no evidence of sexual activity. The person with them had also been in the room on and according to the evidence, before the night they died. Anyone?"

It was Quinn again who raised a hand having found a little more confidence. "Could they be in those rooms by invitation, sir, placed there like?"

It was April who answered. "Until we know who this third party is we're at a crossroads. It's a good point though. Do we know who booked the rooms?"

There was silence.

"I'll see it's checked."

"So, if…?" Cyril looked again at the officer.

"Quinn, sir."

"So, if Quinn is correct, they both might have known their killer." Cyril quickly changed tack. "Escape rooms… what do we know regarding the two men?"

Harry, who was leaning against the wall chewing the end of his pencil, raised a hand. "We have separate reports. Carruthers has been to three from what we can ascertain, Leeds, Newcastle and one in Bradford. The dates are here and are recent. We've no record of Van de Meer being present with him but he could have been booked in under a different name. Each facility has CCTV in the rooms but it's not recorded, it's purely for support during the game and to ensure those playing are safe and that nobody nicks anything. They tell me cameras are less intrusive than windows. One company is thinking of recording the events but a CD will only be given to those participating. The entrance and Reception have CCTV and some keep records for forty-eight hours, whereas one keeps them for four years. We have those here. They came through this morning after a good deal of searching and co-operation on their part."

Harry picked up the remote and the large screen turned from blue, containing the North Yorkshire crest, to black before the grainy images were displayed. "These are stills."

"It's taken some time to find these images as neither man was the lead name on the booking. What we have here is the person we believe to be Carruthers with two others. This is from the Manchester rooms."

"Don't they need the names of all the group for health and safety?"

"If you book a group to play five-a-side football you only need one name who takes responsibility. The same applies here. One person signs the form accepting the company's terms and conditions."

"Do you have the name of this business?" April asked.

"IQ Escapes. When I rang them initially I was informed that a *secret agent* would speak to me shortly. It's role play with a capital R, believe me. They immerse you in the experience and I can see why it might become addictive, challenging and very competitive. Those organising come from a theatrical background and so they know how to create the spaces to reflect authenticity."

April wrote down something that struck her from what he had said. *They immerse you in the experience and I can see why it might become addictive, challenging and very competitive.*

"The room wasn't booked in Carruthers's name. Booked under a Colin Boardman. What I believe to be significant is that Van de Meer and Carruthers went to the same escape rooms but not at the same time. One went with friends one week and then the other the following week and vice versa." He paused as if giving them time to catch up.

"So, the same friends went twice?"

"No, look carefully. The people with them are different. I'm aware the images are not the best quality." He paused allowing them to watch as the images played through a couple of times. "So, the question now is, do you see what I see?"

Chapter Fifteen

There was something about The Stray, especially at this time of the day that made one glad to be alive. On looking up the blue sky demanded more than a brief glimpse. It was streaked with curving lines of cirrus cloud that appeared dragged and smudged informally across a giant canvas, clearly complementing the straight trails of high vapour left from a passing jet. Scenes such as these needed savouring; time to watch the slow but subtle changes. To the observer there was clearly something harmonious about the silent collision of man and nature way above in the heavens. "Beautiful but it will all be gone in a moment, lost forever."

The traffic was busy along the peripheral roads but within this open space the thrum was more soothing than annoying. A dog barked to the right of the path as its owner scooped up a tennis ball and launched it into the distance. The dog, turning swiftly, barked loudly and set off after it at a pace.

All life was here, each person going about their business at a different pace and for varying reasons. It was clearly special. No matter what the season it always had something to offer.

Walking away from the path, the dew, still lingering on the long grass, was of no concern as the green, wooden hut was his immediate destination. The building had the appearance of a large ice-cream stall and was positioned just away from the junction of West Park and close to where Montpellier Hill came into view. As long as one approached from the rear one would be out of view from those on the roads and the main pavement. Even though the small building had windows around every side it was not easy to be seen. Besides, this task was only going to take a minute or two.

***

Harry was clearly both excited and frustrated. "Don't you see? Manchester one week and Leeds the next for Carruthers's group, Leeds and then Manchester for Van de Meer's, same venue, alternate weeks. It was as if they were having some kind of competition. There was some kind of rivalry."

"That's clever," announced April. "They challenge each other and compare scores. What did you say a while back? *Addictive, challenging and very competitive*, right? When was this?"

"Last one was the week before they were killed, the week before they came to Harrogate."

April laughed. "It's staring us in the face. If they were good friends why book rooms some distance apart? If I were going to a convention with a colleague I'd either be in the same place or pretty close by. I certainly wouldn't book accommodation so far away."

"Good point, April, and well done, Harry. Who was the lead name for Van de Meer's group?" Cyril asked.

Smiling Harry replied, "Booked under the name of Colin Boardman." He allowed the information to sink in. "Yes, same as the other group."

"So, who's Colin bloody Boardman when he's at home?" Owen asked. "I'm beginning to smell a rather large rat."

April was quick to interrupt again. "How did they pay for their entertainment?"

"Cash in all cases."

"Didn't they need a deposit when the booking was made?"

"Apparently not."

"Facial recognition on these players?"

"That's the next step. Can we justify the cost, sir?"

"Boardman may well be a false name. I'll clear it," Cyril promised, tapping the pencil against his cup. End of round one. "Thanks."

***

Holding one of the ears to the back of the hut, just above the window and near the centre, he positioned the inner part of the auricle facing downwards. Squeezing the trigger on the staple gun, the metal quickly penetrated the stiffening cartilage, pinning the ear to sit horizontally against the cream painted wooden frame. It was attached as if it had grown there, having the appearance and colour of bracket fungus. He placed the second ear at a slight angle and a little higher. Here the wood was painted green offering a greater contrast. The gun triggered again securing the flesh to the timber. They had been pinned at approximately six feet from the floor away from dogs and children but clearly visible as they contrasted curiously with the painted coloured wood.

"Now how long will it take the clever and the curious to discover these I wonder? Let's hope before some hungry bird decides to take the occasional peck," he whispered before turning away and following the slope that would lead to the bottom of Montpellier Hill.

***

Valerie Thew turned the key in the lock and opened the door of the charity shop. The same aroma crashed into her nostrils making her pull the face she must have pulled every time she entered. She had thought on many occasions it was as if someone or something had died there overnight. A quick spray of the air freshener and the smell was masked. She moved through to the back room to hang up her coat and put her handbag safely away. Within moments the bell on the front door rang.

"No rest for the wicked," she mumbled.

***

"It's clear what we need to do," Cyril announced whilst checking the time on the digital clock positioned on the far wall. "Shakti, I want the media news desk to put out a call for this Colin Boardman. Get them to tidy up and release these images. I want it broadcast on the local radio news, TV and in the press. Get them in as many of these escape rooms as you can. Might just jog someone's memory. It should be straightforward to identify him. This Boardman is acquainted with both victims and we know what he looks like, providing he was one of those in either party but then there's no guarantee about that. We can take nothing for granted. I also want photographs of the victims posting on line and on all other available sites." He pointed to the screen. "Do we have recent images of both?"

Harry nodded.

"One last thing. Do we have the address of Carruthers's previous lodgings?"

Stuart Park stuck up his thumb.

"April, take Quinn with you and check it out. As much information as possible, pictures would help. You know what we need. See if they've seen Van de Meer before. You know the drill. Remember too that the hand was deliberately placed where it was bound to be discovered and we can reasonably assume the ears will also be located somewhere. That's my gut talking."

**

Jim West was standing by the door his hands tucked into his jacket pockets.

"Are you stalking me, Mr West?" Valerie asked with a chuckle. "Or are you looking for something in particular?"

"A stalker at my age... goodness me no. My stalking days are over, that's if they ever existed in the first place."

They both laughed. Even though they had been out together there seemed to be a degree of discomfort, a reluctance on both parts to relax. However, the laughter helped to ease the atmosphere.

"I wondered if you'd like to have lunch, or maybe a coffee? As you know it's my games night tonight. I have a detective fellow popping along. It's to do with those murders. They say the killer removed certain body parts. You've read about them in the Harrogate Advertiser I take it?"

"Harrogate used to be such a safe place and now what with drugs and stag parties coming here the place is changing. Happiest place in the UK to live it was at one time and now… Wendy, Bill's wife, he owns the gallery yonder." She moved by the window and pointed as if to emphasise the direction. "Found one of those body parts, a hand I believe, stuck in the eaves of the building in the Valley Gardens, Magnesia Well, you know the one. Imagine that! I wouldn't be able to sleep for a week."

"I'd only heard a rumour. Someone said they found a head so unless I hear it first-hand…" He shuffled with a degree of unease. "Sorry!" He dragged a smile across his face. "Lunch?"

"Sorry, yes. Quite carried away. Betty's will be busy," she said tongue in cheek knowing it was too expensive.

"I wasn't considering pushing the boat that far out, Valerie. I was thinking more of a pedalo trip around the pond… metaphorically speaking, that is. A coffee and a sandwich?"

"Sounds lovely. Gloria comes in at eleven-thirty and we can go then before the rush. Meet you by the Cenotaph?"

"The Cenotaph, eleven-forty. Right, see you then." He turned and left, giving a wave as he passed the window.

Valerie raised her hand and waved back. She brought her hand in front of her face, opening and closing it a few times, then shivered. "How disgusting and to think it happened here in Harrogate too."

Chapter Sixteen

Owen's desk could never be described as either tidy or orderly, but then neither could Owen himself. If one looked carefully enough, there was a modicum of structure to the way he worked. There was ample reference too to the snacks and meals that had been consumed in the previous seventy-two hours, be it in the form of empty wrappers or morsels and crumbs. A small mug printed with bold red letters as if it were written in dripping blood asked in all innocence, *Is it Friday yet?* It contained his new-found favourite confectionery, Uncle Joe's Mint Balls, and it was strategically positioned to one side of his computer screen. To the other side was the only exposed piece of the desk, a small oasis amidst the chaos, but it contained more crater-like rings than the moon, past evidence that this was the location of the myriad cups of tea that had kept him refreshed.

Owen, having pulled his chair away from the desk, had one of the drawers on his knee as he continued his search. Cyril strolled across, the day's newspaper rolled beneath his arm.

"What is it today for which you search, Owen? The Holy Grail, the lost chord, maybe Blackbeard's treasure or is it the winning lottery ticket for last night's game?" He paused and raised an eyebrow. "And when it's found you'll be able to put us all out of our misery and release us from the bombardment of crap society in general wants to throw at our door." He tapped the paper. "Like misogyny and the plethora of other hate crimes you can now report, serious ones, wolf-whistling and the like." Cyril dropped the paper onto the desk bringing to it an immediate and aesthetic appearance similar to that when an untidy garden is covered in snow.

Owen, having put the drawer back, looked up before thrusting his hand deep into the bowels of the lower drawer with the delicacy of a drainage rod forced in to unblock a pipe. He pulled a face as his tongue protruded from between his lips. The operation was becoming delicate and difficult; concentration was clearly needed.

"Online banking password and details," he said between the occasional grunt as his arm disappeared further into the desk until his elbow disappeared. "Thought I'd taped them to the back of one of these drawers. One more wrong attempt and I'm locked out and I need to transfer some cash otherwise it's overdraft time." He pulled another face that conveyed the gravity of the situation perfectly.

"You'll be pulling more than a face after you've read that. Page six." Cyril leaned over to the mug containing the sweets only to pull out an empty wrapper. "I bet you put the empty packets of the After Eight mints back in the box too!"

Using his free hand Owen dipped his fingers in, pulled out a wrapped sweet and handed it to Cyril. "Search and thou shall find, sir, as my gran used to say."

"I can see that from your, let's say, morning exercise. When you read that," he tapped the paper, "you'll need to search not only for your patience and your sense of humour but that part of your brain that controls your anger." He popped the sweet into his mouth, dropped the wrapper into the open drawer and marched off towards his office. "Thanks for the mint."

Owen retrieved the wrapper and popped it into the pot with the others before picking up the paper and turning to the said page.

"Shit and bloody derision! Shakti!" he called.

Shakti's head appeared from the side of a computer screen. "That's me."

"Come and read this and please, please tell me it's not just me and *Flash* who find this total and utter bollocks."

She moved towards Owen's desk before leaning over his shoulder to read the column headline.

Investigating hate crime risks taking police away from core priorities.

"No shit Sherlock. Listen to this, Owen. *Since 2015 hate crimes recorded by police in England and Wales have soared from just over 54,800 to more than 100,000. Really!*" Shakti's anger exploded. "We've fewer front-line officers, limited resources, a downward spiral of officer morale and we have not only to investigate name-bloody-calling but also when some bloody *snowflake's* upset because a builder's wolf-whistled as they passed. And yet real crimes are on the increase and the clear-up rate has dropped. It doesn't take a genius. Let's refocus. We have two victims this week, one has no hand and another no bloody ears but apparently, we should be searching out Internet trolls. It's not what I came into the force for, Owen, not this shite anyway."

"We could all have a brush surgically implanted and we could sweep up as we went along," Owen suggested as they stared at each other until he decided there was only one thing to do. "Have a mint ball," Owen grunted proffering the cup and producing a broad smile. "It's going to get worse before it gets better." He burst out laughing. "You've just got to see the funny side. Remember that force, somewhere down south, I think, or was it Lincolnshire? Anyway, they got a roasting for setting up a scheme where they'd only respond to burglaries at properties with an even house number thereby halving their call outs. I can see this happening soon with the different religions or certain housing estates or town and city areas unless more resources and a more common-sense approach is taken to these so-called hate crimes. If we're not careful we'll see people taking policing into their own hands and with that will come unofficial judge and jury courts and... I don't need to say more. It's trouble with a capital T and it's just around the corner. Mark my words, Shak."

Shakti sighed and shook her head. "Thanks for that, Owen. Just what I needed was someone to raise my blood pressure to the point of triggering a headache." She thumped him on the shoulder.

"I'll make you and the boss a brew. That makes everything right for us northerners, put it right with tea." Owen grinned.

Shakti sloped off to her desk. "Two sugars."

"You don't take sugar."

"I do now."

Within minutes Cyril appeared. Owen held up the small piece of paper. "Is that a clue? Been reading all about these escape rooms. Might give you the missing combination."

"You could say that, sir." Owen looked at the four numbers. "Amazing the trouble you find yourself in when you forget these. Bank card security code! Just about to make you and Shak a brew."

"Sorry, no time. DC Massiah is waiting in Reception…"

Owen looked back, folded the newly found piece of paper and smiled.

Cyril did not need to say anything else. Owen stood and touched his forelock.

"DC Massiah," Owen mumbled almost chewing every syllable as he tucked the paper back into the drawer. "I thought I saw a host of angels when I looked out of the window this morning but knew in my heart of hearts it's nowhere near Christmas." He moved to the door. "Does one simply bow, genuflect or prostrate oneself before him?"

Bennett simply gave him a hard stare and shook his head. "I'd lock that drawer if I were you, after you've saved yourself the prospect of an overdraft."

***

Remembering Valerie's prophesy that Betty's would be busy, Jim stared across at the queue forming along the front of the famous tearoom. Like Swiss engineering it ticked along without rest from opening until closing; if you visit Harrogate, you visit Betty's, as if it were a rite of passage.

Jim could never quite understand why people would sit inside eating in full view separated from the queue by a pane of glass. To him it was like eating in a goldfish bowl but there was never a shortage of people prepared to wait. *The disadvantage of popularity,* he thought.

He glanced at the clock on the round tower that made up part of the stone façade of the building and checked the time against his watch. He was early. Finding a bench, he took a small paper booklet containing the mechanics of the game *Dead of Winter* from his jacket pocket. He intended to demonstrate it to DC Nixon if he turned up for the evening's games night. It was one he knew well but he still thumbed through the rules just to ensure the game would run smoothly. Confusion on his part would surely destroy any confidence and pleasure to be gained in the game. Within minutes he was not focusing on the written word, his mind was elsewhere.

"Guilty pleasures, Jim West?"

Valerie's voice startled him and he dropped the booklet. "I'm sorry I didn't mean to disturb you."

"Miles away, Valerie. You were right by the way. Look across the road. It would be nice to have a few shares in that business." He tucked the booklet back in his pocket. "I know the perfect place."

***

DC Rodcliff Massiah leaned on some shelving, his security ID hanging towards his left arm whilst he chatted to the duty sergeant in the area behind the front desk. Three officers were busy on the computers and room was tight. This was not his first visit to the Harrogate station but for some reason he felt strangely uncomfortable. Both he and the duty sergeant turned, instantly distracted by the sound of the door opening. Owen raised a hand whilst keeping the door ajar with his foot. Massiah shook hands with the sergeant, lifted his jacket from the coat hook and walked towards Owen.

Clearly standing at six feet five inches tall and equally broad, Owen noticed that the man's biceps filled and stretched the fabric of his short-sleeved shirt, his dark, ebony skin contrasting starkly with the white material. It was rare for Owen to meet a colleague who was taller than he and one who clearly demonstrated that he worked hard at developing and maintaining his fitness.

Moving towards Owen, Massiah slipped on his jacket. He instantly noted Owen's heavily creased shirt, his tie, loose at the neck and haphazardly stuffed into the shirt breast pocket along with his ID card and lanyard. Immediately his free hand swiftly checked his own tie was straight.

"DS Owen?" A huge smile broke across Massiah's lips at the same instant his hand appeared from the sleeve of his jacket and shot towards Owen.

"Thank you very much for coming down to Harrogate. Good run?" Owen said as Massiah instinctively ducked as he went through the door.

"No problems… came the scenic way."

Within ten minutes they were sitting in Cyril's office.

Massiah thought he knew why he had been called but he was mistaken. "You've seen the main report and the initial forensics from the inspection of the garage? It was really immaculate. Surely I can't tell you much more as it's all in the report."

"Just want to pick your brains. It may be something and nothing. I wanted to talk it through face to face so thanks for taking the time. You were born in London but your family's from the Caribbean?"

"Barbados. My aunts and uncles still live in the parish of St James, the most beautiful of parishes. I go on holiday there occasionally. Went a lot when I was a kid but…" The same smile that had greeted Owen resurfaced. "My grandfather was a police inspector, stationed in Holetown on the west coast. He used to take me to look round the station. Put me in the holding cell too. How he'd laugh. That's one of the reasons I became a police officer."

Cyril smiled. "No better reason, Rodcliff. I'm sorry if this sounds bizarre but owing to the nature of some of the games and certainly some of the model figures found in the garage, I just want some information about the history behind them. I know the idea of zombies originated in your part of the world, the Caribbean, and wondered if it features in Bajan folklore. Voodoo and zombies and the like?"

It was clear from Massiah's expression that he found the question was not only baffling, but totally unscientific. However, he had the grace to keep his face straight and he considered his answer with care.

"Ghost stories, Detective Chief Inspector, ghouls and ghosts and things that go bump in the night. The true origin of the idea of the zombie is from Haiti, as I'm sure you're aware. Pins in dolls, the keeping of parts from the dead whether that be hair, their finger or toenails, teeth or even parts of their clothing so that they can become the living dead. In Barbados we have a malevolent spirit called a Duppy, same in Jamaica. My folks would tell me if you put your umbrella up in the house you'd bring the Duppy. Like we say in England, putting the umbrella up in the house will bring you bad luck. Another piece of our widely believed folklore tells that if you approach the crossing of four roads at just before midnight there would be a Duppy and the steel donkey waiting to entrap you. The donkey was even more evil than the Duppy. It had eyes of fire and breathed flames too whilst rattling the chain that was wrapped all around it. Folks would wait until after midnight to approach those roads."

Owen was fascinated and stared at Massiah as he spoke.

"Many people say they'd seen the donkey but no one could really agree on a true description. Same with graveyards, dangerous places. You'd hear that there would be a Duppy living there just waiting. From my understanding, everyone can make up some kind of story to frighten the naïve and the young. In my opinion it was done to keep the curious and the kids from going where they shouldn't. In London, my mum used to frighten me away from going near our local ponds and canals by talking about Jenny Greenteeth; she was successful too. I never learned to swim."

Cyril glanced sideways at Owen. He tried to imagine the person in front of him as a timid child but failed to even get close.

"I see why you've asked, though. From what I've been able to find out, a good number of the games introduce the idea of the zombie. They feature pandemics and world catastrophes, nuclear and chemical changes to humans, transforming those contaminated after death to become the living dead, maybe a malevolent spirit. There are examples where the world is attacked by alien forms, many, as you say, taking the guise of zombies. I think the connection is very insubstantial." He glanced at both Cyril and Owen.

Cyril was impressed on two levels, firstly the confidence with which Massiah spoke and secondly it was evident he had a firm interest in the case, obviously triggered by his time at the garage.

"I know you're familiar with the two murders and that body parts were removed from each victim. We've located the missing hand of one of the victims but not the ears of the other. And as you say, parts of the deceased are kept for ceremonial purposes." Cyril could feel his idea slipping away and Massiah's reply, *But here in Yorkshire, sir?* seemed to hammer the final nail in the coffin for Cyril. "Maybe you're right."

"However, what if some game player sees himself as a Duppy, a zombie for some bizarre reason and plays a new game using his own rules? Those rules might or might not be understood by the others within the game. Seeing all of those things within the garage room suggested to me he wasn't just your standard gamer. You have there a true fanatic. Maybe he was bored with the run-of-the-mill games and looked for a more challenging and exciting venture, a game with high stakes. And what about the skulls?"

Cyril looked across at Massiah. "We're keeping a truly open mind. Now please let Owen show you round our own Castle Grey Skull. Appreciate your coming down. I'll call on you again should we need to if that's okay?"

He stood and shook Cyril's hand. "Pleasure and thanks for..." he paused, "the invite. If I can be of further assistance, I'd be more than happy. It's an interesting case, sir. Good luck."

Cyril sat back down and doodled on his jotter. He had managed to retrieve a leather desk blotting paper pad from Newby Wiske when the old police headquarters was closing down. Most things were put up for auction but this came as a gift. In place of blotting paper he had inserted paper. He simply wrote... *someone thinks he's a Duppy!!!*

Chapter Seventeen

Quinn drove taking the shortest route to Richmond and although relatively new to the Harrogate team he seemed assured. "Love Richmond, ma'am, something about its position, the castle and the like. Green Howard museum too. My great uncle, if that's what my granddad's brother is, did two teaching practices in the primary schools here when he was studying to be a teacher. He's retired now. I came with him last year and he pointed them out. One's now become posh apartments. I could see him travelling back in time as he stood where the playground used to be. Wonderful thing, the memory."

Turning onto Newbiggin, the car slowed as it travelled across the cobbled surface. Richmond was certainly beautiful. Rows of stone-built houses flanked either side, each individual in its own right. Most had a height and a distinctive façade of their own, bringing originality and charm to the straight street.

"It's up by the church on the right." April pointed.

"No need for sleeping policeman with these cobbles. Maybe Harrogate should bring them back. It'd certainly slow down the traffic," he suggested as the steering wheel vibrated frantically in his hands.

Quinn parked the car facing into the kerb under one of the many trees that also lined the road.

Both climbed out and Quinn rested his elbows on the roof as April looked at the numbers. "It's that one."

***

It was clear to Jim why the café he had chosen did not have a queue stretching from the door and down the street. The lingering smell of fried bacon seemed to hang heavily in the air

111

giving a constant suggestion that the day was younger than it was. He knew that he would carry it with him on his jacket for the rest of the day. However, Valerie did not seem to notice and if she did she was far too polite to say.

"I enjoyed the other night. Can we do it again sooner rather than later?" Valerie sounded sincere.

"How does Friday sound?"

"That would be lovely. Must use the facilities." Valerie paused and looked around as if searching for the appropriate door. Jim pointed the way and smiled at the use of the term. He had not heard that expression in some time. He finished the rest of his coffee. When she returned, he stood. "You dash and I'll pay."

"Already attended to, my treat and thank you for popping into the shop this morning. Looking forward to Friday. Where do you fancy?"

He took Valerie's arm. "Just you leave that to me. Do you like surprises?"

She raised her eyebrows. "Sounds wonderful if not a little mysterious. What is strange, is that I'm accepting these lovely offers but I know nothing about you."

He laughed. "What can I tell you to put your mind at rest, even though we've been out in the past and you arrived home safely?"

"What did you do before you retired?" Valerie sat again and Jim followed suit.

"I worked in theatre, originally London and then Leeds and I even did a stint here in Harrogate."

"An actor?"

"A jack of all trades, as you have to be. It's not all standing ovations, lights and makeup. There's a lot of donkey work backstage. After that I opened a business here, picture framing. However, I couldn't compete with IKEA and the like but that's a different story."

"You had a shop?"

"I still do a bit but it's now rented. Gives me a return each month so I can treat people I like to dinner."

Valerie put her hand on his arm. "You must tell me more on Friday I'm intrigued."

She stood, smiled and left. "Must fly."

After a few minutes Jim came out of the café. The Stray beckoned. On reaching the Cenotaph he saw the flash from the blue strobe lights, bright even against the noontime sun. The two police vehicles were parked on the pavement at the top of Montpellier Hill. Moving across the road he passed the boules pitches built in an endeavour to bring the town closer to Europe. They were empty. Brexit might see them revert to gardens and benches. Only time would tell.

Pausing, he could see the tape stretched from the police vehicle around the side of the green hut before travelling some distance to the rear. It was then wrapped around a trunk before crossing the path, round a second tree and back to the second of the two cars, thereby including the wooden building. Jim thrust his hands in his pockets before moving across the road. He glanced sideways and saw a white and blue tent to the rear. A figure dressed in protective clothing emerged before speaking to a woman standing next to a police officer just within the boundary tape. He walked on and found the first available bench; it gave him a clear view and he was away from the group of curious bystanders.

Shakti had seen the man sit and stare but turned as the CSI approached. She listened and made notes as she spoke, her mask still covering her mouth.

"Human, too. I've checked against the images we have from the post-mortem and from what I can see they match. Don't tend to find many ears pinned to places these days. It's a ritual that didn't catch on."

Shakti could see from her eyes she was smiling, the crow's feet gave the game away.

"The gentleman who found these is in the police car. You might want to interview him. We should be finished shortly. Checked the ground for shoe prints and the close surrounding area as per usual but that's all we can do. As you can imagine in such a public place…"

"Indeed, you do the impossible." Shakti thanked her and approached the police vehicle.

The officer opened the rear door of the Range Rover. A man was sitting looking at his phone.

"Mr Clark?" She smiled. "DC Misra. Bit of a shock for you."

"Dr Clark," he corrected her. "It's not every day you confuse human ears for bracket fungus." He laughed out loud. "Thought the historic building had fallen foul to rot. I was clearly misguided. And if you see the funny side it gives a whole new meaning to the saying, *walls have ears.*" He smiled and raised his eyebrows watching the expression change on Shakti's face. "I'm not easily shocked. I understand this to be the second discovery of lost body parts, if the press is to be believed." He held up his phone and Shakti could see the photograph he had taken. "It was this small silver skull earring that gave the game away. Actually, that's not strictly true. Once I'd moved closer it was apparent that it wasn't a fungus. Thought it to be a practical joke but on closer inspection I knew immediately that the parts of the ears were real. Now why would anyone do such a thing?"

Shakti was surprised by his demeanour, it was as if it were a normal daily occurrence. "You seem very calm about it, Dr Clark."

"I'm a clinical scientist."

"Right, I understand your reaction now. I just need to take a brief statement and check your contact details. I'm grateful for your help today and for your time."

"You have your work cut out DC Misra, what with two intriguing murders within the same week. I believe there are links with the gaming convention. I noticed too the police website and the bulletins posted. You have my utmost respect."

Shakti jotted down his statement and requested he delete the photographs on his phone.

"Now, if my services are no longer required it's a quick coffee and back to work."

Jim watched with interest as the female officer moved away from the police vehicle. He then noticed the man climb from the rear and shake the officer's hand before making his way towards Parliament Street.

Within fifteen minutes the tape would be removed and this small part of The Stray would return to normal, apart from the odd curious members of the public who continued to observe the scene.

The entertainment over, Jim also moved away.

***

The recently discovered ears were removed for forensic examination and the photographs taken on site were now sitting on Cyril's desk.

"Got on like a house on fire with DC Rodcliff Massiah. Don't know what I was expecting but he's a good bloke. Arranged to meet him for a beer on Saturday. Said he had a game he'd like to show me." Owen grinned.

"I sincerely hope it's innocent and nothing to do with the living dead." Cyril looked up and grinned. "I can see why you like him. You're both from the same mould, Owen. You don't see a copper your size every day of the week. I think he'll go far. He seems efficient and keen, a bit like yourself. Always said you're as keen as mustard."

Cyril slid the photographs across the desk. "Common denominator, please."

Owen studied the photographs again, paying particular attention to the earring. "The skull. Made me think immediately of Carruthers's shelves."

"According to the boffins, that was placed there after the ears had been removed. If you recall, the other lobe was left in situ. They believe that this might have been deliberate to allow the insertion." Cyril tapped the skull on the photograph. "We know the lobe still present had a piercing that hadn't been used for some considerable time. Whoever killed these two is playing some kind of game, not only with these players…" He again tapped the photograph. "… but with us. He's the virus, the alien or zombie. He might even be Massiah's Duppy but he's controlling the game and he wants to see if we can stop him."

Owen was not accustomed to his boss being so dramatic and it shook him a little. "How can we be players if we don't know the mechanics of the game he's supposed to be playing?"

"We need to find those players from the escape game. We need to locate our mystery figure and organiser, Colin Boardman."

***

"We simply didn't see eye to eye, DS Richmond." There was a pause that seemed to linger too long. "If you don't mind my saying so it seems strange to be confronted by a Miss Richmond when here we are… in Richmond itself."

"We should thank our lucky stars it's not April as that's my Christian name."

Quinn turned to look at his boss and then back at the seemingly elderly lady nursing a cat and a cup and saucer on her lap. He simply smiled.

"Was there a serious issue between you and Carruthers?"

"My husband initially thought it a good idea that we rent the apartment we have attached to this building. Originally this was my mother's home and when we married, she kindly let us have the flat. Sadly, she died in a tragic accident. What she was doing on the stepladders at her age we will never know. I was out shopping and when I returned there was a note to say she'd been rushed to the hospital but sadly…" She allowed her hand to stroke the cat before taking a sip of tea.

"So, you then took the house on her passing?"

"Yes. We kept the flat in case friends or his brother came for the weekend but as my husband said, it was empty ninety per cent of the time and when he retired it seemed sensible to rent it out."

"So was Kevin Carruthers the first person to rent?"

"We tried holiday lets at first but that was just hard work. You'd never comprehend how some folks leave a place. No, that didn't work and so we advertised locally. Within a week Kevin had looked round and put down a deposit, his first month's rent on the flat. He was with the Co-op, if I recall, an apprentice."

Quinn was growing a little frustrated and wanted to ask why they had fallen out, where her husband was and what were the finer details of her mother's accident, but he knew his place and remained silent.

"So why did he leave?"

"He was told he must leave. We suddenly kept noticing people coming round in the evenings and staying until all hours. I don't know if I should say this but, put it this way, Kevin wasn't the masculine sort." She paused and looked at both officers in the hope they would understand. "You know." She put out her arm and lowered her hand. "A little limp of wrist we used to say. I thought he was up to no good, a knocking shop my husband called it. After a while we confronted him. We used to check the flat initially but it was always immaculate and so we stopped. Well, we had the shock of our lives when we went in. One room was painted totally black, black! I kid you not! There were cabinets full of the most disgusting creatures and a row of skulls on a shelf that would fill a graveyard. Gave me the willies I can tell you."

Quinn could not resist a smile and received a subtle tap on his foot from April.

"Did he explain?" April knew just how to extract the information at the correct pace for Quinn to note down.

"Games, he didn't have a TV, strange boy, but played games. He wanted us to believe all of these callers were other members of the gaming group. He apologised and said that he'd no idea he was causing upset and he would look for accommodation elsewhere. We just accepted his offer and

117

gave him a month's notice. He didn't need it as he moved out within the week."

"When was this? Did you know where he went?"

"Must be over a year. My husband left not long afterwards, about thirteen months I think. How time flies. Tempus Fugit. I think Kevin took further lodgings but I can't tell you where."

April shot a quick glance at Quinn.

"You say your husband left too?"

"Yes, a week or two after Kevin, maybe it was even a little less than that, one forgets. We hadn't really been seeing eye to eye for some time, probably since he retired, always under the feet and a bit of a bully if I'm to be honest. I don't know if I should say this but…" She paused. "No, if that got out I'd be embarrassed. I reverted to my maiden name when he'd gone. Brooke. Felicity Brooke."

"And your married name?"

"Boardman."

April turned quickly to Quinn. "Notify Bennett and then come back."

"Have I said something wrong?"

"No, not at all. May I call you Felicity?"

"Of course, but I'd prefer Fliss."

"Fliss, three things, firstly did your husband leave you for another woman?"

"Woman, goodness me no. Let's just say he liked being with the boys."

April was perturbed and it took her a minute to get her thoughts in order. "Did you rent the flat after Kevin or had the experience been too disturbing?"

"I didn't rent it again, in fact, I didn't touch it."

"Finally, I'd like to show you some photographs and let's see if you recognise anyone."

Fliss put her cup and saucer on the small table and pushed the cat from her lap. "Now let me see these photographs."

Chapter Eighteen

For Alan Bowen the day was dragging; Tuesdays offered nothing. The weekend seemed so far off. He recalled the game in Harrogate. It had been close. He then thought of the character in the pub. Dipping his hand into his pocket he brought out the blue figurine he had given them. His phone signalled that he had a message.

We met in the pub the other night in Harrogate. You said you were keen gamers. I've a friend with the ultimate escape room. You don't just get an hour you get longer but the stakes are higher too. Still interested? Meet me on Saturday by the library steps on Victoria Avenue at 7.00pm. Just you. If you're unsuccessful we'll challenge your mate at a later date. No need to reply to this message as you'll either pick up the gauntlet or you'll not show, either way, no hard feelings. I've booked you a room at Grants B&B on Selby Drive. Sorry, you'll have to pay for that but it's cheap and cheerful. Check in after 3pm if you wish to take it. Remember, if you're successful the celebrations will be massive. If you work Sunday, you might want to book a day off from work too! Make a note of the time, place and accommodation. Don't tell David. Call him if you're successful and offer him the same challenge.

Good Luck!

P.S. Bring the figure I gave you as it might be one of the clues.

Bowen reread the message before fumbling for a pen and writing the date, time and name of the accommodation on the back of his hand.

Within five minutes the message had been removed.

***

"Quinn, sir. We're in Richmond at Carruthers's digs and we've just found out the name of Carruthers's landlord is Boardman. DS Richmond instructed me to notify you immediately and that further info would follow as soon as we have it." Realising he should have asked for a Christian name too he had to think on his feet. "Hopefully we'll have a photograph and we'll post as soon as."

Back in the lounge, Fliss perused the pictures. "That's Kevin without a shadow of a doubt. He seemed such a lovely lad at first. How is he?"

April paused surprised by her question. Kevin's murder had been in all the papers. "He's dead, Fliss. He was murdered. That's why we're asking about his past. I just assumed…"

It was clear from the expression on her face that she was totally oblivious to Kevin's demise. At that moment Quinn returned.

"Is everything okay, ma'am?"

April nodded.

Quinn looked across at Felicity Brooke and then at April. "I'm sorry to have to ask you this but do you have a photograph of your husband and can you tell me his Christian name?"

Felicity looked older than she had minutes ago. What was going round in her head was anyone's guess. She returned Quinn's gaze. "I do and his name's Colin. He's not killed him has he?"

Both April and Quinn felt a flush of excitement and that emotion clearly contrasted with that of their interviewee.

"We have no reason to believe he has anything to do with the case but we do need to clear him from the investigation." They waited for Fliss to collect herself and focus her thoughts.

"He certainly had enough of a temper on him but he usually managed to control it. He trained in the army as I'm sure you're aware. Now, where did I put that horrible man's photograph?"

***

Every time Alan Bowen thought of the challenge his stomach fluttered. He had tried to retrieve the message but it had been deleted. It made him think of James Bond. *Read and memorise, 007, then dispose of this message*, he said to himself trying to mimic Sean Connery's Scottish twang. If he had needed anything to alleviate the boredom then such a challenge was beyond what he had imagined. *To win and then challenge David to beat his time was just the icing on the cake,* he thought. He checked his watch. Should he tell David that he had been the chosen one, the one to lead or should he just do it and inform him when he was successful? He would consider the situation.

***

April had photographed the picture of Colin Boardman and sent it to Bennett via her phone. She then checked the notes Quinn had made. "I wasn't expecting that, Quinn."

"Me neither, ma'am. How old would you put her at? The cat on her knee made me think of a grandmother but then grandmothers can be in their thirties these days."

"Fifties, possibly, my guess would be early to mid. Looking at the photograph I assumed Colin to be older having been retired some time, but that could have been taken a year or two ago. We'll soon have those details when the census is consulted. Last known whereabouts…" she read the notes. "Here we are… lived around the Harrogate area or possibly Pateley Bridge. What area does that cover, Quinn?"

They sat in the car, reflecting on the meeting.

"A lot." He stared down the road. "Pretty place to live this. These properties must be worth a bob or two."

"Not another woman she seems to think."

"A man? Thought that straight away when she said he'd buggered off almost immediately after Carruthers left. Whoever it was I hope they had more brass than this Ms Brooke. My dad retired at fifty-five."

"Sorry?" April put the notes on the dashboard.

"He could be about fifty-five, Boardman. As I said my dad retired early. He'd saved sufficient funds and he'd had enough. Can't blame him. I'll go as soon as if the money is right."

"No, about the man?"

"It was just when she said he'd gone. They'd lived under the same roof for ages as the flat was integrated. She wouldn't have known if something was going on. She didn't seem to know much about what actually killed her mother!"

"You might have a point, Quinn." She noted it.

Quinn started the car. Glancing back at the house April saw Felicity Brooke watching them from the window. She was not hiding the fact she was there. It was then Quinn saw her raise a hand and wave. Instinctively, he waved back. "Funny woman that."

"Knowing what I know about our two victims and trying to weigh up Ms Brooke, there may be more to Kevin's leaving than meets the eye."

***

On their return, the information regarding the Boardmans was already up on one of the boards. The census had revealed two people living at the Richmond property and that Colin Boardman was ex-military. His forces' records, also presented, showed that for some time he had been stationed at Catterick Garrison. It was assumed his proximity to Richmond was how he and Felicity had first met. Felicity Boardman was registered as a housewife. Their ages were fifty-eight and fifty-three years respectively. They had lived on Newbiggin since 1997, married in the same year and prior to that she had lived in the property with her parents. His parents had divorced when he was twelve and since then he had lived with an elder brother in York.

"Probably drifted into the army as a teenager," Quinn suggested as he fingered the attached sheets. "Wonder if he went to the army training college, the one out Penny Pot way?" He thumbed through the records. "Yep. Here it is, he trained in something to do with the signals. It was then called the Army Apprentices School when he attended. Didn't stay for that long. He transferred for further training to Catterick. Medical discharge in 1981. It says see medical records. Do we have them?"

"If we have, they'd be there."

Quinn flicked through the sheets of paper. "Nope, not here."

April went to the phone on the desk. Within minutes she returned. "Should be with us by the end of the day. More initiative is needed, Quinn."

Quinn was unsure whether that was a mild chastisement and looked at his notes. "What about his brother...?" His voice tailed off as he saw Bennett and an officer enter. His question had fallen on deaf ears anyway.

Cyril walked in with DC Dan Grimshaw.

April smiled. "Find him in the car park, sir? I recognise him but can't say I remember his name. Didn't he used to work here?" There were a few chuckles.

Grimshaw had been on annual leave but had then fallen off a stepladder whilst pruning a tree in his garden, necessitating a further month off.

"Welcome back. How's the leg?"

Grimshaw held up both arms. "Wrists, plural. Not easy, and certainly not pretty. You find out fairly swiftly who truly loves you when you're incapacitated in such a way. I didn't see many people rushing from this office in my hour of need but I'm grateful for all the cards and the odd bottle." His smile said it all and it was clear for all to see he was happy to be back.

"Funny that."

"What's funny?" Cyril looked at Quinn.

"That's how Felicity Brooke's mother died. Fell off a stepladder..." he left a suitable pause. "Allegedly."

Although the comment was not lost on both April and Cyril it was on Dan.

"I've missed the sincerity and warmth of this place."

Cyril had been looking at the boards during the conversation. "April, please make sure Dan's up to speed. I'm away for a couple of days from tomorrow and..." he did not finish. "Boardman, still nothing? No address? Collection of money, pensions? Use of credit cards or bank? Phone calls? Did we get his mobile number from..." he paused. "Felicity Brooke, Boardman as was?"

"Small army pension goes directly into his bank. That's all we know. The manager gave us no further information other than there's been nothing drawn on the account since before the two murders. However, they did say and I quote, *A significant amount was withdrawn two weeks previously.* We only managed to ascertain that because it's a murder enquiry and we were concerned for his welfare. Sometimes this data protection makes getting relevant information more difficult than drawing bloody teeth. However, they have agreed to watch all transactions on all accounts, even Felicity's, in case he's using hers."

"He's either being supported or he's dead," Grimshaw interjected, his tone quite matter of fact. "Man cannot live on bread alone." He winked at Quinn and smiled. "Have we met?"

"Something else you'll read in the report. He may have been having an extramarital relationship before he left Richmond, male or female, we have nothing as yet to say either way." April smiled. "Now, DC Quinn, known now as Quinn, meet DC Dan Grimshaw. Shake his hand but be careful, we've only just got him back." April winked.

Cyril stepped in. "We're looking at CCTV and cross-referencing not only with facial recognition technology but also some experimental Super-recognisers who, they tell me, are highly skilled in analysing and therefore comparing unfamiliar faces. They'll be starting with the images captured from the escape rooms. We'll then move on to those taken on the night of the murders. Maybe he was at the convention or simply out and about. It may take time."

As Cyril left, April turned to Quinn. "Stepladder, that's initiative, another example of your clever thinking. Find out the circumstances of her mother's death. Check if there's a coroner's report." She touched his elbow and smiled. "Good work, Quinn. Jolly good work."

***

He ran a hand along the painted surface. The delicate use of stippling had given the wall a look not only of age and dirt but also wear, as if it had been occupied by many a prisoner. The graffiti, scratched and drawn, gave a reality to the room's décor, as did the pin-up pictures set at rakish angles. Some were worn and torn whilst others were defaced. The small shelf of books and the white toilet bowl in the corner, installed to be functional, also gave an air of authenticity and there was nothing here that would not have featured in a cell used in the seventies. It had to be remembered that many were the legacy of the Victorians. The door was not heavy, not made from steel but the clever use of paints and laminates gave it a convincing appearance. The concave viewing window, however, was now replaced with a small camera, one of three positioned covertly within the room. It would all be observed, it would all be recorded. Why else go to so much trouble? After all it was only a game!

There were three other small rooms created within the building. The green mile, the area just outside the door, was tight and dark. Lights positioned along the base of the wall clearly emphasised the deliberate use of old, green linoleum. Although only metres in length it led to two doors. The way the player interpreted the questions and the clues would determine which door they would enter. One door contained a large warning sign. Dimming the lights, adding the smells and then the sounds would be the final touches.

"That's years of experience, skill and a good eye for detail. Not everyone can do that." He left the cell door ajar as he checked both rooms at the end of the corridor. All was ready. He extinguished the lights.

Chapter Nineteen

As Cyril drove, Julie was reading and her father was sleeping. The M62 had been the usual stop start on account of the fog. The farm house positioned between the lanes, known on the radio traffic reports as *the little house on the prairie*, was barely visible. Drivers seemed to defy weather conditions and drove purely on instinct. However, away from the Pennines the visibility improved and the sky cleared.

Once off the A500, Cyril estimated the journey would take only another fifteen minutes. He also knew that Wendy, his step mum, whom he now considered to be his mother, would have the sandwiches and cakes already on the table. From the messages he had received, he knew she would have been looking forward to seeing them. He could almost sense her excitement.

Wybunbury Lane was so familiar. It was as if each tree, wall and fence had been there for ever and he could no longer understand why he had stayed away for all those years. His regret washed over him in waves.

The wheels crunched the gravel and the red-brick house beckoned. As the car pulled up in front of the door, Wendy appeared, immaculate, diminutive and wreathed in smiles.

"I didn't expect you for another hour." It was her way of making them feel at ease as they were running late. That was Wendy. She hugged Julie and her father but lingered when it was Cyril's turn. She moved her hand to his cheek. She said nothing but she sensed the drive had been difficult. "It's so good to see you, Cyril. I miss you."

"Lovely to see you…" There was a momentary pause but it was soon corrected. "…Mum. You look radiant." He bent and kissed her on both cheeks.

A tear appeared in the elderly lady's eye and she was neither embarrassed nor concerned by it. "So, you've decided to have your father's Bentley?" Her voice did not conceal her uncertainty.

"Julie's father is going to, let's say, baby-sit it for me. I neither need it nor have a garage for it but he does. Besides, he has time on his hands and he also loves to tinker. I'll use it on sunny days and special occasions. More importantly, I have some news."

Cyril watched as Julie and her father went through into the hall. He dipped his hand into his pocket and brought out a small ring box. He flipped the lid. It was empty.

Wendy put her hand to her mouth and then back to Cyril's cheek. She smiled. "I have it safe, as promised."

"What are you two up to? Not changed your mind, have you, Cyril, about..." she paused and winked "... the Bentley?"

Cyril laughed. They moved inside and closed the door.

Within an hour the afternoon tea things had been cleared and the doors to the large garage were opened. There, sitting beneath two tarpaulins in the semi-dark, was his father's gift to him, his treasured maroon Bentley.

"Pick a date between 1946 and 1952. Its year is on the registration document. Ancient might be the correct term," Cyril muttered with little reverence.

"May I?" Julie's father looked at Cyril eagerly before removing the covers. "Classic, Cyril, classic. They don't make things like this any more. Hand built by real craftsmen who took pride in their work. This wasn't assembled by some faceless robotic tool."

He watched as the fine filigree of dust burst skyward like illuminated myriad atoms suddenly released into the light. The now exposed deep maroon body and the huge radiator looked foreboding. Cyril stood back and watched as her father's hand fell lightly on the bonnet, a tender, cautious caress as if the car were alive and had feelings. He was sure he saw his lips move as if introducing himself.

"She's beautiful, Cyril." He quickly removed the second sheet.

Within twenty minutes the car was running, released from the trickle charger, tyre pressures and oil checked and a ghost of a grey wispy smoke curled from the exhaust.

***

Harry Nixon crossed The Stray heading for his games night. His umbrella was occasionally caught by the gusts of wind that seemed to come from different directions. The resultant changes to the force of the rain proved both difficult and annoying. This inconvenience seemed to increase his reluctance to be part of the evening. Not only was it the weather that seemed to conspire against him, but also the unknown. He realised that in his heart of hearts it was the thought of wasting an evening being bored to death. Hours of playing Monopoly suddenly came to mind. Once across The Stray, the rain seemed to relent and drive in only one direction.

Jim West had sheltered under the veranda of the jeweller's situated behind the Cenotaph. It offered perfect protection from the rain and provided a clear vantage point. He had spotted the poppy umbrella well before Harry saw him. They had agreed this rendezvous as it was perfect no matter what the weather.

Harry waved as he approached before lowering his umbrella. "British weather! Excuse the flash and bright design." He pointed to the umbrella. "Bought in support of the Poppy Appeal. "

"Firstly, Harry. May I call you Harry? Thank you. May I say what a difference your having a word with your colleagues has made. I noticed a number of officers have called and let's say the atmosphere in the passageways has improved tremendously." Jim touched Harry on the shoulder. "Now, come along, the Fairfield Hotel is just along here as you know. We use one of the rooms they reserve for functions. The beer's good too."

Within minutes they were entering the hotel. The room was busier than Harry had imagined. After dropping their coats, Jim accompanied Harry to the bar before they went round the room stopping briefly at each group of players. A variety of games was being played by a mix of players, young and old, male and female. Each table or tables depended on the number of participants, specialised in one game. The room was bright and from his witnessing the games room in Carruthers's garage, he expected things to be different. He also immediately recognised some simple family games and felt less intimidated. On one table two people sat chatting as Jim and Harry approached. Harry was introduced. A board was set out before them. Harry's anxiety quickly returned as in front of them was a number of different sized boards, different cards and figures, all of which seemed rather sinister.

"We're going to introduce you to this game, it's fairly straight forward."

Harry picked up the box lid. "*Dead of Winter*, sounds utterly... friendly." He then picked up one of the figures. "Not a particularly happy looking character."

"They're known as a standee but I call them figures especially when they are as good as mine. We'll each control a small group of people who have different skills and who come together to survive a zombie apocalypse in the worst of winter conditions..."

Immediately on hearing the word *apocalypse* Harry's feeling of uncertainty returned and he could see the photographs of the two murdered men in his mind's eye. He tried to concentrate on Jim's swift run through of the basic rules but key words kept sticking in his mind. *Morale* and *betrayal* made him feel particularly uncomfortable.

"We're going to play a three person game. You and I play the first game together and as you're the apprentice on this occasion, with a limited knowledge of the mechanics of the game, we'll be allowed to move away in order to discuss our next strategy. Remember, one of these guys might just be a traitor within the colony. Is that okay?"

There was another word, *traitor*. He quickly glanced round the room. There was a sense of competition with a sporadic laugh and odd expletive but it seemed fun. He sipped his beer.

"And for all we know you might be the traitor, Harry," one of the other players announced as he shuffled the cards, looking directly at him without a hint of a smile. "We'll all have to be on our guard."

Harry sensed the hairs on the front of his arms rise and he suddenly felt extremely ill at ease.

"We'll also stop the game to explain anything should you wish. Remember, we all had to start at some point." Jim's smile seemed genuine and reassuring. Harry relaxed a little as the game began.

***

The dinner had been wonderful. Wendy had prepared a risotto. She knew it to be a favourite of Cyril's and now they stood together in the kitchen. He had insisted he did the clearing and the loading of the dishwasher and besides he wanted time alone with Wendy.

"So, you've finally decided to ask her? I'm so pleased. She's such a beautiful and kind person, darling…" she stopped in mid-sentence… "or have you done so already and if so, did she say, yes?"

Cyril pulled a face as he turned to look at her. He moved closer and kissed her forehead before depositing some suds from his finger onto the end of her nose. "Mum used to do that when I was nipper in the bath." He paused a moment as if that memory of a lost time returned momentarily. He could almost smell the water lingering with that of his mother's fragrance; he could almost feel her wet hand on his young skin and sense his mother's love.

Wendy could sense it too. "Your mother was a very special lady, Cyril. I know she'll be alive as long as you're on this earth." She raised the glass she was holding. "To the past, my best boy and now to your future."

Cyril dipped his hands back into the water.

"Bless you." He paused as she held her glass to his lips so he could also make the toast. "Cheers." He took a sip.

"Proposing? I've tried, goodness me I've tried to ask Julie. To pop the question but…" He went on to explain.

Wendy laughed out loud when he told her about his plan to surprise Julie in the Asian restaurant.

"But there's no ring in the box!"

It was Cyril's turn to laugh. He rinsed more plates in the soapy water before putting them in the dishwasher. "There was a curtain ring, huge it was too, because I know you said you wanted me to have my mother's ring. Julie would've understood."

"God works his magic in many ways. Maybe that was fate. Knowing Julie, she'd have held it up to her nose and snorted."

The laughter in the kitchen attracted both Julie and her father. "Is there a party going on in here?"

Cyril and Wendy pulled a straight face before turning to look at each other. Wendy winked at Cyril. "He was trying to teach me how to suck eggs, Julie. I've never washed up correctly before, did you know that?"

***

You could never say that Harry had seen the light but by the end of the evening he had a much clearer and more informed opinion about the games played. He also had an understanding as to the importance of the various figures. They had gone through the game twice and Harry had managed to play his own group of people on the second run but the zombies quickly took control. Jim, however, seemed totally dominant. Harry had deliberately asked for a few minutes at the end to chat about escape rooms.

"Like a book, Harry, they're similar yet different. You might like reading but you might prefer only one or two genres but you can read others too. Gaming and escape rooms could be classed as just different genres. It's about winning, following rules and using experiences of other games and strategies to triumph or to escape. It's about finding clues and then solving the puzzle they bring, a bit like your line of work I imagine."

"Do you enjoy both?" Harry asked as he finished his beer and offered to buy Jim another. He refused politely.

"I'm not a fanatic, Harry, but I do enjoy trying to keep the old grey matter stimulated. I love the interaction and I've always enjoyed creating and solving puzzles. I've beaten the time at the new escape room here in Harrogate. It's a franchise so the clues are not the most difficult to unravel but it's a great way to pass time with friends."

"Are they all franchises?" Harry asked as they collected their coats.

"Don't forget this." Jim held the poppy umbrella.

"How could I possibly?" It brought a smile to his lips. He liked Jim. Although he had initially felt reservations, after the evening he had warmed to him.

"No, some people go it alone in this business, risky if you ask me as I personally believe it to be just a craze. The best are those who are gamers but also who have had training in the theatre. They display a greater imagination and therefore there can be a real drama and atmosphere about the way they design and set up their rooms. Basically, each game carries a star-like rating, and from my experience that rating is given depending on the number of puzzles you need to solve to escape. That might indicate you're in one room but it might mean that you have to move through a series of small rooms to escape. The more rooms you have to enter the more difficult the experience is. Some even hide the way out."

"Time being of the essence I take it, so they can't really be too difficult, impossible like?"

"Indeed. Like life, Harry, there's a balance. If it's too easy, nobody would return and the business would fold, yet on the other hand, if it's too difficult… It has to be a challenge and it has to be seen as fun with friends and beating a system or team building. Businesses use them for that very purpose and it has to be better for kids than sitting at home watching television or playing those computer shoot 'em up games. At least they invite interaction."

"Sounds interesting."

"I've been working on a project but I promised not to talk about it just yet. One day I'll hopefully show you in the not too distant future but if you and a friend would like to try the escape room I could go with you." Jim seemed to anticipate what Harry was thinking. "Don't worry, I'd just watch how you and a friend solved the puzzles to escape, or not as the case may be. If you do, however, it will have to be later rather than sooner. You could always try it without me."

Harry did not know what to say. If the truth be known this was unpaid overtime and he had been doing far too much of that lately.

"One more thing, I really felt welcome this evening and I'm grateful to you and your group. There was, however, one bloke playing with us…"

Jim held up his hand. "Stan," he nodded. "Stan's quite a balanced chap; where most people might have one chip on a shoulder, Stan's got a chip on each. Stickler for rules as you might have noticed and ultra-competitive. To be honest, he's not well liked. Thanks again for helping with the smokers."

Harry's walk back home was kinder than his journey into town. The rain had stopped and the wind was now but a zephyr. He stood waiting to cross Parliament Street and suddenly felt hungry for the first time that evening. The red tail lights from the passing cars illuminated the still wet road in blood red lines. He immediately thought of the zombie standee he had held earlier, all claw marks and blood. The smell of kebabs seemed to find his nostrils, a siren's call to his stomach and an attacking force against his willpower that seemed to immediately wave a white flag. He turned and followed his strongest sense. Another lost game of will.

***

Julie was asleep when Cyril came to bed. He had listened to, 'The Lark Ascending' and held the violin his mother had so deftly played. The haunting yet optimistic strings had filled the room with what seemed to be a warmth and a joy. He tumbled the small, blue box in his hand as if it were a die. As the music stopped and the room took on a more solemn air he leaned forward in his chair and slowly lifted the box lid. It now held a ring, a classical, period design from another age but breathtakingly beautiful. He removed it, instinctively bringing it to his lips. "Bless you, Mum. May the wearer of this ring have your love, kindness and selfless forethought." He felt the tear move down his cheek and he wiped it on his sleeve. "You're turning into Owen," he whispered trying to regain a little control.

Returning the ring he closed the lid. "Cyril Vaughan Bennett it's time you went to bed. Tomorrow is an important day."

Chapter Twenty

Owen took the morning briefing whilst Cyril was absent but there seemed to be little to report. They had still not located Colin Boardman's whereabouts but they had tracked down the lodgings Carruthers had used up to the time he moved into his new apartment.

April spoke after the introduction. "Carruthers started sharing a static caravan, the ones that look like cabins, near Brompton-on-Swale. It's a short commute to Richmond. We have no definite dates as he actually wasn't the owner and I think it was a mutual arrangement between them. The owner, Gary Drakes, has lived there for two years and before that he rented a cottage on the local landowner's estate. He was a gamekeeper and general dogsbody but left that job prior to moving into the caravan. From what we've been able to ascertain he terminated the work of his own accord, he wasn't fired."

There was the odd groan.

She smiled. "No pun intended but it proves some of you are listening. However, we have only made tentative enquiries. The caravan's not been searched or investigated forensically. We'd like to keep Drakes where we can find him until we know more."

"So how come he knew Carruthers? Was he a friend?" Owen asked before standing and moving away from his seat towards the noticeboards. He let his finger roam over the printed sheets before stopping. "Carruthers's brother, Richard. He's in the same game… Shooting Ground Administrator, now whether that's similar to the role of a gamekeeper I'm unsure but we know that he organises shoots, we presumed purely clays but you just don't know. Brian…" Owen turned to Brian

Smirthwaite. "Give him a call and see if he knows or has heard of this chap, Gary Drakes. We have his number."

Brian left the room.

"Wonder what Carruthers did with his three bikes, skulls and all of his boxes of games?" Quinn questioned. "It's a lot of stuff to keep in a caravan especially when it's not yours in the first place."

"Am I right in thinking you can't live in these places three hundred and sixty-five days a year? They have to be vacated for a period so they aren't classed as full-time homes." It was a voice from Owen's right.

Owen raised his eyebrows and pulled a face conveying that it was a relevant question to bring up. "Give the campsite manager or owner a ring. Find out what they know. If you think it'd be worth a trip out there then inform me and I can organise it, but just enquiries, mind. Whoever calls might be his long-lost mate trying to find him." Owen winked. "Get the picture? Let's keep him where we can find him, as April so rightly said."

"What about John Van de Meer? It all seems to have gone quiet on that front apart from finding his ears." There was definitely no pun intended from Shakti.

"From the investigations so far nobody, including his parents, seemed to know that he was in Harrogate during that period. He had indicated that he was going away for a few days. He didn't leave an address. It was the school holidays so nothing unusual there."

"Nothing from Forensics other than a definite match. The skull earring was added post mortem, another clue handed to us on a plate, a bit like the indecipherable writing on Carruthers's hand. The fact that they were both found attached to..." Owen paused and a number of others in the room understood the reason. He whispered in April's ear. She immediately flicked on the large flat screen positioned on the far wall before Googling the name of the campsite. Within seconds a number of heads had turned and the image of the so-called caravan appeared.

"Comments, please!" Owen barked, excitement was evident in his voice for the first time that morning.

"The hand was discovered at Magnesia Well pump room and the ears were pinned to the wooden chalet type structure just on The Stray at the top of Montpellier Hill. Both are follies."

"To be honest, the well building isn't made of wood, it's constructed out of stone," Harry observed.

Owen was quick to respond. "There is, in my opinion, a connection bearing in mind the architectural style. The body parts were left or attached to locations that were similar, as the hand was located in the wooden, ornate eaves. That caravan-type cabin has all the features of both locations, what with the eaves and its style. Is our killer trying to tell us something or lead us in the opposite direction?"

"Our English word Folly comes from the French word folie meaning foolish in the sense of buildings such as these."

Owen looked at April and smiled.

"The dictionary also mentions that the word Follies is a theatrical venue with glamorous female performers."

There was a silence broken only by Brian's return. He waved a piece of paper, the smile on his face conveying a degree of optimism regarding his telephone conversation. "Sounds a lovely chap, Mr Richard Carruthers. Wanted to know when his brother's body will be released. Gary Drakes worked with Richard a good few years back when they were both youngsters. They worked together in Scotland, training as keepers. To be honest, he thought he'd been injured in a shooting accident. Supposedly received a compensatory payout and then left. Hasn't seen him since and was surprised when I mentioned Kevin. They knew each other back then but he didn't seem to remember a friendship, Kevin being a little younger."

"Get a picture of Drakes over to him and get a definite ID. I take it we do have a fairly recent photograph of Drakes?"

"As yet, no. Prelim enquiries," April replied as she switched off the screen.

"Quinn. You'll be making the trip. I wonder if they have any for sale or for holiday rental? Maybe you could find a young lady downstairs who might like a trip out to accompany you. Make it more realistic." Owen smiled. "Don't scare the bugger off as he might just be the guy we're looking for. Shakti, just run this Drakes guy past Van de Meer's parents to see if the name rings a bell… it's a long shot but for the sake of a call by the Family Liaison Officer it might be worth a try. Mention Boardman, too."

Owen took a moment to collect all his papers. "Thanks very much. Anything else?"

"There's one thing but it might be nothing."

It was Dan Grimshaw who stood. "I've been looking over the case with a fresh pair of eyes for any small clues. I was fascinated by the flat and garage belonging to Carruthers and so looked at the inventory taken of his possessions. The large and beautifully framed pictures drew my attention but it wasn't what was on the front but what was on the reverse. All were framed in Harrogate and held a label, *Westside Framers, Harrogate.* There was a phone number but it's been discontinued. Registered to a Jim West."

"I know him. He had a framing shop and he's also a gamer so they must have known each other through that I assume. I'll get onto it."

***

The Bentley was washed and the first coat of polish was being applied to the maroon paintwork. The chrome had been buffed and it mirrored the blue of the sky and dazzled as it caught the light. Considering the car had stood for so long it was in remarkable condition.

Cyril had been late out of bed. The cup of tea which Julie had brought to him earlier was still untouched. Drawing back the curtains he stared at the garden. Birds darted in and out of the foliage and he allowed his eyes to drift up to the copse of trees on the hill. He had climbed it many times as a child. Looking back at the empty bed he had this sudden yearning to climb back in. How he would love to just spend the day cocooned and secure but today was to be a busy one.

Once dressed, Cyril went out to the car. The yellow garden hosepipe lay across the gravel like some motionless serpent with its tail disappearing into the barn-like garage. Fred Pritchett simply smiled his greeting. His sleeves were rolled up to his elbows as he continued to buff one of the rear mudguards with a degree of enthusiasm that would have put a younger man to shame. Cyril walked round the car stopping at the front to admire his handiwork. "You must have been up at first light to get this sorted, Fred. I have to say you're doing a fabulous job. Had breakfast yet?"

Julie and Wendy watched from the kitchen window.

"How I wish that his father had been more like Fred. Don't get me wrong, he was a good man and worshipped Cyril but you never saw them interact the way he does with your father."

"Maybe that's because he's not his father, he's more a friend or even an equal. There's no rivalry. Neither do I see any jealousy from my father. They've always just got on."

They continued to watch and were taken aback when Fred threw the duster over his shoulder and the two men embraced.

"Now what are they up to?" said Wendy, concealing what she knew that Julie did not.

"In my profession I might know every working organ of the human body but that's when they're cold on the table. When breathing and warm, the functioning of the human male completely baffles me. All this over an old car! I'll sort out the breakfast."

Wendy giggled and touched Julie's arm as she moved away from the window. It was then that Wendy spoke quietly to herself as a warm inner feeling brought a further smile to her face. "I do love you, Cyril Bennett. If only your mother could see you on this important day. I shall write about it in my diary to her this evening. She'd be so proud of you. Your dad would too."

Julie only heard the final few words. "Sorry, didn't catch that. Dad would be what? What on earth are those two up to now?"

"It's nothing, just an old lady wittering to herself as she does most days."

***

The clock on the dashboard showed 11.21 as Quinn pulled into the campsite. He had phoned ahead and found that two of the cabins and one static caravan were available for rent. Reception was situated a short distance from the road entrance to the site.

"Remember the story, a surprise holiday for my parents, as simple as that. Drakes's place is number four." Quinn had looked on Google Earth and had an idea of the site layout. He could not, however, determine the numbers of the specific caravans.

They walked into Reception and introduced themselves.

"You're keen. Didn't expect you so soon." The middle-aged lady facing them had the reddest of cheeks and her hair was tied up in a bun. She looked, as far as Quinn was concerned, the quintessential farmer's wife. "I have two to show you, one of our luxury cabins and one of our more cost-effective static vans. Is that alright?" She did not wait for an answer. "The statics are the less expensive option as they're set away from the river. Still good views but... the cabins, or chalets as folks call them, overlook the river and are beautifully equipped. Some guests say luxurious in their reviews I'm pleased to say."

As they walked along the path, Quinn spotted chalet number 4. He paused as if taking in the view of the river. There was someone on the balcony leaning on the railing. A wisp of smoke from the cigarette held in the man's hand drifted back over his head before vanishing. The river was shallow at this point and the water on the shingle rippled like a whisper. Trees on the far bank allowed the light to pierce the heavy foliage in pin-straight rays, dancing on the peat-tinged water as if accompanying the river's voice. It was stunning.

"What an idyllic setting," Quinn announced as he turned to the receptionist, who seemed eager to move on.

"You can see why the chalets are so popular. The evenings are spectacular as you can imagine, particularly when we get the deep red sunsets."

"Do you get biting creatures, mosquitoes and the like?" the PC who had been co-opted asked in all sincerity.

"It's the countryside, dear, and you're near water. In the evenings in the height of summer we do, but it doesn't detract. We get few complaints."

Quinn turned to wave at the man he assumed to be Drakes but received no gesture in return.

"That's Mr Drakes, been here a while. Bought that when we first set up. Selling was the plan then but we realised that renting was the better option. He knows we'll always buy it back for a good price. He's happy enough living here, but who wouldn't be looking at that view and to be honest he keeps himself to himself. In fact, he helps us with the wildlife, conservation and the like. I'll point out the nesting boxes he's put about the place."

"Would you mind if I took a picture?" Quinn asked as he moved his partner nearer to the river, at the same time ensuring the man on the balcony was in shot.

"Be my guest."

"Smile!" He took a few pictures allowing the camera to swing round whilst zooming in. It was an opportunity not to be missed.

"My father's a keen cyclist, nothing flash but he loves trundling about. Is there a place to store bikes?" Quinn asked in all seriousness.

"We've a secure store for bikes but most people chain them to the railings by their accommodation. Now let's look at what you've come to see."

Within half an hour they had viewed the accommodation and were heading back to Harrogate.

"It's like being in a Bond movie, Quinn. Did I do alright?"

Quinn just turned and smiled. "Perfect."

Chapter Twenty-One

Cyril's phone crept along the kitchen table as it rang and vibrated. Wendy picked it up and saw the caller's name. It was Owen. She handed the phone through the window. "Cyril, it's Owen. He must be missing you already!"

"Owen, you still in *Grey Skull*?"

It made Owen smile knowing that his boss had adopted his nickname for the police station. It was most unlike him. "Going soon, sir. Hope all's well and you've been able to rest. Quinn's managed to get a photograph of Drakes, the guy Carruthers was living with. Sent it to Richard, his brother, for a positive ID. We're also checking Drakes against the images taken from the CCTV footage. Thought it was worth a punt but your Super-recognisers are going to be busy. You back tomorrow? I'm off tomorrow but in on Sunday. Meeting up with Massiah... Beers at his local, taking Hannah too. See you Sunday. Looking forward to seeing you here in that Bentley. You'll be just like Morse."

"Jaguar, Owen. Morse drove a Jaguar and there's a subtle difference in make if not colour but then... See you Sunday."

***

Valerie had fussed about with her makeup longer than at any time in the last twelve months and she was still not satisfied. "Mutton dressed as lamb, Valerie Thew. You should be ashamed of yourself." She stared at the face in the mirror and pouted before running a finger along her eyebrow. "Old age and poverty. What says you, Monty?" She turned to her cat, which continued to lick the inner thigh on its back leg. She sighed. "Men!"

Jim West waited under the same veranda as he had done when meeting the police officer for their visit to the games night. How the time flew by. He looked at the familiar busy scene and imagined that it would all carry on the same long after he passed away. *Would anyone remember me like they remember those names carved into the Cenotaph?* he thought as the strains of 'Don't Cry for Me Argentina' sung by a busker round by the church echoed from the surrounding walls. It was a hollow, plaintive cry that was neither in tune nor particularly subtle. "Have music done away with, some of these folk," he mumbled to himself.

"Talking to yourself, Jim West? Penny for them." Valerie tapped his elbow. "The last time I met you here you were miles away. Dreaming of the night that lies ahead or saddened by a life that's gone by?"

"I guess a bit of both." He leaned down and kissed her on both cheeks.

"Very theatrical, kind sir." She noticed he was wearing a brown checked bow tie. "The tie is lovely."

"Come, I have a table booked."

***

Owen left the station and was dropped off at the *Coach and Horses* where he had arranged to meet Hannah. He needed some company and he craved a pint. The pub was busy as usual with no music, games, children nor animals; that was the ruling and the atmosphere of a traditional pub was better for it, therefore attracting not only Owen and Cyril, but many who valued good conversation.

Hannah found a table in the corner as Owen went to the bar. He noticed a regular, Geoff Blakesley, deep in conversation and sent over a pint before returning.

"So, what do you suspect, Hannah Peters?" Owen raised his glass. "Cheers! Thank goodness it's Friday."

Hannah pulled a quizzical expression. "Sorry?"

"There's something going on. Flash has been like a cat on hot bricks recently. A while back when he was taking Julie for that Asian meal, he couldn't settle. Grumpy as hell too. I couldn't do right for doing wrong. It's either Liz who's come back to haunt him again, and Christ I hope that's not the problem, or…"

"Or what?"

"I hear church bells. I'll need a best man's suit and you, my lovely girl, will need a bridesmaid's frock."

It was as if the pub was suddenly yet metaphorically silenced. Hannah was so shocked upon hearing the word *bridesmaid* she choked on her drink and sprayed a fine mist of gin and tonic in Owen's direction.

"Marry?" she announced with enough volume to make the barman and a number of regulars turn and stare. Geoff, who had recently received the pint, raised it and shouted his congratulations.

Owen simply put his head in his hands before standing. He raised a finger and now the pub did fall silent. "Not us. Don't get all excited, particularly you, Geoff. I've not just proposed. It's a friend of ours who's been married twice before and he's hoping it'll be third time lucky. That's why Hannah was shocked."

Geoff smiled and held up his half-empty glass before suggesting, "I think the gentleman protests just a tad too much."

There was a great deal of laughter as Owen sat back down before announcing, "I need another beer."

***

The restaurant had been quiet for a Friday but then they had eaten early.

"Are you doing your valuable charity work in the shop tomorrow?" Jim asked after wiping away a morsel of cheese from his lower lip. "You ladies do a marvellous job. Tell me, do you notice the strange aroma in that shop of yours or is it something you just get acclimatised to?"

"You never get used to it and strangely it never seems to go away. Marjorie, you know the big lady, she seems to think it's either damp or a problem with the plumbing. What about you, Jim. A quiet weekend or are you playing games?"

"I've some things to do in the old shop. I've also some framing to do for a friend. I'm pleased now I still have the space to be able to do it. I won't have for much longer."

Valerie looked puzzled. "I'm sorry, but I thought you said you had rented it, the shop?"

Jim flushed a little. "Can you keep a secret? This cheese is lovely by the way. Are you sure I can't tempt you?"

For the first time since they had met, Valerie felt a little unsettled. Jim could sense the change in her demeanour.

"I do, I still have a small area at the front but that will soon be put to use. I'll have to sell my equipment or find a small lock-up garage. Well, you know my love of games, Valerie, and my knowledge of theatre? I'm going into business and I'm so excited by the prospect."

Valerie relaxed a little, leaned across and took the small piece of cheese from his plate. "Business?" She popped the cheese into her mouth. "This cheese better not give me nightmares, Jim West, or you'll be in trouble. What sort of business?"

"It was all serendipity really. I rented the flat to Colin, he'd had marital issues and needed a break so he took a short-term rental on the apartment above the shop. Anyway, we got talking one evening and I mentioned escape rooms and that I'd like to make one for individual players. There are a lot of general games played solo, take solitaire for example, people play it constantly, the crosswords in all the papers and sudokus as well. People like to challenge themselves as individuals. Gamers are even more competitive but I had the idea of making this one, my game, a bit more of a challenge. As you know my background is in the theatre, it's what I know... putting on a show." He sipped some of his port before nibbling the cracker. "Anyway, because it's my shop I put up some of the capital, Colin is ex-military so he invested and did all the logistics. He took responsibility for much of the heavy labour. I did the paintings, the Trompe l'oeil." He then explained its meaning.

"So apart from Trompe whatever you said, what exactly have you done?"

"We've made the first one person escape room game. It will be the most challenging within the north east." He finished the last of the cheese.

"We could walk back that way and I could show you the place if you'd like. I'll text Colin to let him know so he won't worry; he still rents the flat. We've already done a few trial runs during the games convention week. We found a few punters who were keen to give it a go. Mind you, people always will when it's free. From what they said to Colin they think it's going to be a success."

Valerie suddenly felt a tingle run down from the back of her neck.

***

The row of shops looked stark in the artificial street light of mid evening. The Harrogate streets seemed busy as people hurried in both directions; it was Friday night and the start of the weekend. A number of shops in the row displayed signs showing they were either *to let* or *for sale*. It was a sign of the times for many town centres.

"As you see, Valerie, not the best of times to set up a business. That was one of the factors that made me take the plunge. I'd tried to sell the shop but there were few takers." He removed the keys from his pocket and unlocked the shutter protecting the door; that covering the window would stay down.

Valerie was immediately struck by the compactness of the first room. Filling the space was a sloping table covered in carpet, two machines, one having the appearance of a small 'v' shaped guillotine, and a large upright table containing some cut picture mounts. She also noticed a few sheets of glass leaning against a far wall. On a rack along the ceiling were lengths of picture frame mouldings and resting on the horizontal sections of the partition wall were two unusual looking staple guns, other tools and pieces of small equipment. She looked at Jim.

"This junk will all have to go and it will be converted into a Reception area. It's through here where the gamer will be briefed."

Jim opened the door made within the temporary partition wall. They entered another room. This was about the same size as the first but was well painted. Only a small table and two chairs graced the room.

"We've tried to make it look like a police interview room. I hope you didn't recognise it as I presume you've never been inside one," he chuckled.

She shook her head.

He opened a door to the side. "This is where it begins. Come in. I think you'll know what this is meant to be."

Valerie was staggered and laughed out loud. "Jim West, it's a real prison cell!" She held onto his arm as she looked around the room. "It even has its own facilities."

They both laughed.

"Those in this room are supposed to be troubled and penitent, not shrieking with laughter."

The voice made Valerie jump and Jim felt her nails dig into his arm. "Bloody Hell!" She turned to look at the man standing in the doorway.

"Colin. Thought you'd be out with that mate of yours. Valerie, meet Colin. Major Colin, meet Valerie."

They shook hands and Valerie apologised for her French. She really wanted to tell him he had nearly scared her shitless but thought it neither appropriate nor in character.

"Going in ten. What do you think, Valerie?"

Letting go of Jim's arm she looked directly at Colin. The hairs on her arms seem to stand up and she felt a tingle run across her shoulders. A sudden chill seemed to envelop the room. It was her Svengali gift. *Major?* It was her first thought. She did not think so. "It's different. Trompe l'oeil if I'm being honest." Sometimes she surprised even herself.

"Must fly. It was lovely to meet you, Valerie. We have another trial tomorrow evening so we'll run it as before." He smiled at Jim and waggled his fingers to Valerie as if in a wave and quickly left, closing the door behind him.

Valerie immediately saw that there was now no door, simply a wall. It was quiet and she sat on the bed.

"Are you alright?"

She nodded. "I think I'd like to go home, please. I've had too much excitement for one night."

Jim put his finger into the gap to try to pull open the door but quickly moved away holding his hand. "Hell!"

"What have you done?"

"Nothing, sorry, a splinter up my nail." He put his finger into his mouth and sucked. He could taste the bitterness of his blood. "There's only one thing for it." He turned and smiled at Valerie. "We need the big guns!" Removing a penknife from his pocket and tucking the blade into the gap he prised open the door. "Good job Colin didn't pop the bolt across or we'd have been here all night!"

Chapter Twenty-Two

Owen had not only found his match by sheer size but he now realised that Rodcliff had the capacity to enjoy a few pints of real ale too. Hannah had dropped him off at *The Moon* in Thirsk, Rodcliff's local, while she went into Northallerton to do some shopping.

They had both enjoyed their first meeting at the station and when Hannah had suggested she was intending to do some shopping in Northallerton, Owen had organised to meet him at the pub. As they stood at the bar Rodcliff ordered the drinks whilst Owen surveyed the room. The atmosphere was warm and friendly. When they entered it had amused them both how there had been a sudden and noticeable drop in volume as people stopped chatting and heads turned in their direction. Looking along the items behind the bar, Owen did not fail to notice the ceramic painted bottle in the shape of a skull on one of the shelves.

"Bloody haunted by skulls. Everywhere I seem to go there's one staring at me."

"You'll feel better after this." Rodcliff handed over the pint.

Within a minute Owen found himself staring at a board game the like of which he had never seen before.

"Warri, Owen. A game that originated in Africa but was brought over to the Caribbean with the slaves. Barbados was, as you know, famous for its rum and the board is made to look like the top of a rum barrel. These..." he pointed to the grey seed-like pieces "...are *knicker* nuts, sometimes called *sparkies* as Bajan kids would rub them against a stone and they'd spark and get hot. They'd then hold them against someone's skin and burn each other!"

"Friendly game. Good to see kids are the same the world over. We used to give each other Chinese burns. Grab the wrist and twist in the opposite direction. It was a challenge to see who could last the longer without calling out."

"I did that too. These are the seeds of a plant that grows close to the sea and they're as hard as iron. The idea is to win as many as possible and the one with the most at the end of the game is the winner."

"It's in a pub over here?" Owen sipped his beer depositing a white froth moustache across his upper lip.

"There was nobody more surprised than me when I saw it but to be honest, they were not playing it correctly. They are now!"

It all looked far too confusing for Owen. He stared at the board and the two rows of five bowls below which was a larger single bowl dug out of the wooden top. He took another drink as if to summon up some inner courage.

"That's your bank." Rodcliff pointed to the large carved bowl in the wooden top. "Place them there when you win the seeds. We'll play slowly so don't worry." Owen's frown told Rodcliff all he needed to know.

Hannah had been standing watching for some time before Owen noticed her. He stood as she walked over and he introduced her to Rodcliff. "This is warri and I've just won three games in a row." Owen sounded pleased. Rodcliff winked at Hannah.

He stood. "May I get you a drink, Hannah, seeing I'm the loser so far?"

Hannah smiled. "Sparkling water, please. No ice." She moved closer and ruffled Owen's hair before kissing him. "To the victor the spoils."

"Bet you can't guess what these are called?" Owen's enthusiasm was almost childlike. He held up one of the grey seeds.

She pulled a face and lifted an index finger to her lips giving the impression she was deep in thought. "Magic beans?"

Owen laughed. "Knicker nuts… honest. Ask Rodcliff."

"I believe you, Owen."

"I'll show you how to play." Owen's enthusiasm bubbled.

"Lovely… how very exciting." Her sarcasm was lost in the beery haze.

***

Alan Bowen left Harrogate Railway Station and leaned on the fencing running along Station Parade. The small garden area opposite surrounded an ornamental dome-topped folly. It was familiar to him and brought his recent visit to mind. "Game, bloody, on!" he said to himself as he retrieved his phone from the depths of his jeans pocket. He had logged the details of the B&B into the maps app and now he only had to activate the icon. It showed his present location and the route he needed to take. According to GPS it would be a five-minute walk. Checking the time on the phone he realised he had an hour before he could register. Food was definitely next on the agenda. Looking up the road he saw a Zizzi restaurant and decided this might be the best place in which to eat and to take stock.

The restaurant was busy but he was soon shown to a table. He had brought with him a notebook containing the jottings he had made after each visit to the numerous escape rooms. On turning the pages memories flooded back. He paused at one, a venue in Paris. They had even elected to try using the French clues. It had been a disaster but they had spent a highly amusing evening there. It was not the recollections for which he searched but the finer points, the details he had jotted down of the clues and memos of the ways they had been concealed within each room. He had added small diagrams between the writing for clarification as an aide-memoire. On reflection there were a number of experiences with remarkable similarities.

"Are you ready to order?"

Alan had not even looked at the menu.

***

Valerie had been sitting at the table, rolling the napkin ring in her hand for a while. She stared at the phone uncertain as to her next step. Monty had been more than content to stay on her lap. Never before had she felt such a strong sense of revulsion upon meeting someone for the first time. Everything about him seemed suspect. She closed her eyes. His title, his demeanour, his voice, his sincerity and worst of all his friendship and relationship with Jim seemed somehow false. The theatre that played in her head appeared confused. Normally she could penetrate the initial blur and focus on people within their true surroundings, but the fog persisted. She knew that she could not risk voicing her concerns to Jim.

"Goodness what would he think of me, Monty, the eccentric woman from the horrible smelling charity shop who also has this gift. She can tell what people are really like from looking at them, she can see behind the powder and makeup. No, there's only one thing for it. Mummy is going to have to grab the bull by the horns."

***

Blood dribbled from under the nail as the tweezers tried to grasp the offending splinter. It was becoming infuriating. He neither had the time nor the inclination. His phone rang, adding to his annoyance.

"Is that Jim West?"

Harry Nixon's voice was immediately recognisable. "Good morning, Harry. You've just caught me."

"It's business I'm afraid. Do you recall framing some large pictures for a Kevin Carruthers?"

"No, doesn't ring a bell. What were they?"

"Posters advertising games. One was a zombie, black and white."

"Posters? Yes, yes, I remember. They were framed using black and gold moulding with non-reflective *True View* glass, which protects from ultra violet light damage. Looked great when they were finished but that's of no interest to you, sorry. Those were not commissioned by a Carruthers, they were ordered by an undertaker, a Mr Duffers."

"Are you certain, Jim?"

"Yes, did them not long ago. It was the name Carruthers that threw me. I used up the last of my business stickers on the back. They were a house-warming gift if I remember correctly. Collected in a long black limo late one Friday. I'll have the date somewhere if you need it."

***

The incident room was empty apart from a slight electrical hum that seemed to emanate from one of the computers but it was neither annoying nor disruptive to April's thought processes. She in fact found it comforting as if she were not alone. For some irrational reason, it made her think of Liz Graydon, a colleague who had been murdered in the line of duty. She basked in her memories. She checked the details back from facial recognition and the interview with Richard Carruthers, who had immediately recognised Drakes. She looked up his number and dialled.

"Am I speaking to Richard Carruthers?" She could almost sense the sigh at the other end of the phone.

"Speaking. What is it now?"

"DS Richmond, North Yorkshire Police..."

"DS Richmond, the fact that there is no number registered on my phone and the way that you've been pestering me for some time gives me a clue as to who you are when my phone rings. Now, believe it or not, I'm trying to co-operate fully but I've work to do here. What is it this time?"

April moved the phone fractionally from her ear. "Just one point I'd like to clarify, it will only take a minute. You mentioned that Drakes was injured, an accident you said, and that he received some compensation. What do you know about this incident? Was he officially compensated or was he paid to keep matters away from legal proceedings and then possibly the papers?"

"I wasn't present on the occasion of that particular shoot but it's what I heard. We were, at the time, pestered by the bloody do-gooders, the animal rights brigade who seemed to love intimidating those paying to shoot. They'd dress in a very threatening and aggressive manner with full masks and hidden faces. By the way, the police were helpless. I was going to say useless but that would, under the circumstances be rude as I'm sure their hands were tied. The fact is that the bloody birds and the countryside wouldn't exist without the landowners and their breeding and nurturing of sporting birds but that's a story for another time. Anyway, Drakes was with a small group of beaters heading out and they were confronted by this mob, that's what they were. I believe there was some pushing and shoving but that was all until later when Drakes was discovered to be missing at the end of the day's shoot. They found his priest and his game clapper later, in the area where he was last believed to have been seen."

"Priest?"

"A weighted stick used to despatch injured birds humanely. It had his name etched into its handle as did the clapper. That's used to make a lot of noise to bring birds to flight."

"Do people often go missing on these things?"

"Occasionally, some amateur beaters get genuinely tired, wet, cold and fed up and just bugger off home. On occasion I've known beaters go for a pee and miss the tractor trailer back. They tend to return after a bit of a hike. Done that myself the odd time."

"How long was he missing in total and were the police involved? I've discovered nothing in our archive."

"Drakes's case was different. According to the gossip he was found badly beaten with some kind of gunshot wound. That's what I heard. I personally never saw him again but then

I wasn't there that long afterwards. I had a better job offer and accepted it. I heard on the grapevine that he'd received some sort of compensation to keep it all hush-hush. It was a strange affair and nothing else was said. I did hear the odd rumour, which seemed to indicate the tale grew with the telling. Unfortunately, that can be the way of country folk. I should know as I've been lucky enough to live and work with them for all of my career."

"Where did he go?"

"As I've already said, I don't know. You could ask Tommy Boardman if he's still alive. He was head keeper at the time. He organised the shoot."

April repeated the name slowly and emphatically just to ensure she had heard correctly. She had. "Thank you very much Mr Carruthers. Your comments have been invaluable."

Putting the phone down she swung back on her chair. "Well, well, Tommy Boardman. We now have a new Boardman. Are you the man I think you are?" she said quietly to herself. "Are you Colin's brother?" She suddenly had a vague recollection of Quinn asking a question during a recent briefing to do with this very subject. She was beginning to appreciate Quinn.

***

Alan Bowen stood at the gate and studied the board positioned between two blue uprights giving details of the accommodation and vacancies. The front door was open but the inner glass-panelled vestibule door was locked. Alan pressed the bell and waited before looking at the leaflets advertising local amenities. There were also some cards placed by local restaurants. He was attracted to one for a Greek restaurant.

The door opened.

"Mr Bowen?"

Alan smiled and entered.

"Welcome to *Grants*. Is this your first time in Harrogate?"

Alan explained that he had visited a couple of times before but this was his first overnight stay. He held out the card for the Greek restaurant; he had passed it on his way. "I've just picked this up. Would you recommend it for this evening?"

She looked at the card. "You look younger than your telephone voice, do you know that? You'll need to book. It's usually busy on a Saturday but I could do that for you if you have a time in mind."

The thought of dining early did not appeal to him; he had not long since eaten lunch. He calculated that if he were meeting at seven, the game, even allowing two hours, meant he should be out by nine. "Would nine-thirty be too late? I didn't book here, by the way, a friend kindly did that for me."

"That explains it and this." She collected an envelope that was propped up by the telephone. "It was left for you today, posted through the door." She handed it to him. "The restaurant? I can but ask." She smiled. After swiping his credit card she collected three keys from a hook just above the desk.

"I'm meeting a friend at seven by the library, the one on Victoria Road, I think. Is it far?"

"Fifteen minutes at the most. Now let's get you organised and then you can relax. Here are your keys. The front door is locked at ten, so that's the front door key. This..." she pointed to a key partly covered with red plastic, "is to this, the vestibule door and this, the largest one on the bunch is your room key. Sorry, but they contain the large wooden key ring to prevent guests from accidentally taking them home. You're in number four as that's what your friend requested when he booked. Is that alright? It faces the sunny side, the front. Let me show you. This way."

The room was as described, bright and quite large. She had pointed out the bathroom and the tea and coffee facilities before turning to leave. "The details for check-out and breakfast are in the brochure on the desk. I'll let you know about Mykonos Restaurant. Be two ticks. Have you come by car?"

"Train."

"No need for a parking permit then." She smiled and left. Within five minutes he had confirmation of his restaurant booking.

Alan sat in the chair by the window and looked down the road. The low sun shining through the green leaves made him screw up his eyes. "What do we have here?" He had an idea that the game was starting. This would either be a welcome note or a clue of some kind. He carefully opened the envelope and pulled out a small paper square.

Welcome Mr Bowen,

I'm delighted you have booked in as that fills me with optimism that you might just beat the system and escape… but then that will depend on you and your expertise. Please look at the puzzle below, it's simple, yes, but then we don't exercise without warming up first. Here, my friend is your warm up.

Until 7pm. Please don't be late.

There was nothing else. Alan turned the paper over before rechecking the envelope but it was empty. He sat back in the chair and closed his eyes allowing the bright light to play on his eyelids. He moved his head in and out of the sun's rays enjoying the colour difference the light brought; the contrast was marked. He then smiled. "Room four, Mr Bowen, the sunny side." He picked up the paper and held it away from the sun's rays before moving it into the pin-sharp light. "As if by magic. Seek and you will find." Taking out a pen he copied the clue which had just appeared on what had previously been a blank piece of paper.

Chapter Twenty-Three

It was either by sheer fluke or pure magic that the Bentley had managed to cross the Pennines and arrive at its new home without incident. Cyril, driving ahead, had cast many a cautious glance through the rear-view mirror anxiously wondering whether the motorway speed would be too much for the old car. Julie had elected to travel with her father believing it might be the only opportunity to take an extended drive in it.

Being alone also gave Cyril time to reflect on the two murders. He felt convinced there was something he was missing and now he was back in Yorkshire, his only familial duty completed, he was eager to return to work. Having possession of his mother's ring made life a little easier. He could also focus his mind on planning the correct time and place. That thought, however, filled him with a fusion of excitement and fear and he did not know which was the more powerful.

***

Quinn entered the incident room and was surprised to see April. She turned and regarded him. He stopped abruptly and tried to think of something he had omitted to do that she had requested of him; it was that kind of look she had cast.

"Coroner's inquest…"

She held up her hand. "I'm impressed with you, Quinn. You asked a vital question, remember? You happened to be ahead of us all and mentioned the word *brother*. And then because Dan Grimshaw came in with *Flash* it was lost in the excitement. Fortunately, Colin Boardman's brother might have suddenly surfaced."

Quinn moved round the desk and dropped the file he was carrying. April perused this latest information as he pulled up a chair.

"Does this Tommy Boardman still work as the head gamekeeper up in Scotland or is he, too, suddenly going to be missing?"

"Waiting to hear. Those wheels have been set in motion. What do we have here?"

"Inquest on the death of Felicity Brooke's mother. I was amazed to see the conclusion given as an open verdict. From what I recall in training, that's an unusual verdict. According to that," he tapped his index finger on the file, "suicide must never be presumed but must always be based on evidence that the deceased planned or exhibited an indication that they might take his, or in this case, her own life. There had been a suggestion when she was admitted to hospital. She'd said and I quote..." He flicked the file open to a page marked with an orange *post-it* note... 'I just wanted it all to be finished... for it to be over and done with.' The court felt that even though she had fallen from quite a height from the tall stepladder, that suicidal intent was not beyond reasonable doubt. Interestingly, it was pointed out that her fatal climb could have been for some other reason."

"Why was the stepladder there in the first place?"

"They were decorating her room. The wording, *wanting it all to be finished,* was possibly a reference to the decorating and not to her own life."

"So why not accidental?"

Quinn just looked at her, knowing full well he had neither the knowledge nor the crystal ball answer she required. "It's interesting to consider who might benefit from the lady's untimely death."

***

Alan looked at the puzzle he had copied from that concealed within the original square piece of paper. He would keep both,

161

not fully understanding how they might be of use once he was locked in the escape room. What he did believe from past experience was that they would be relevant.

```
E  A  M  E  H
P  N  R  C  T
A  A  E  L  Y
C  G  V  E  L
S  E  E  V  N
E  S  R  E  O
```

Having already showered he read through his notebook. He would not be allowed to keep his phone nor any other personal items once the game commenced, that was standard procedure. He picked up the ushabti figure and took a moment to study it. Letting his finger run over the smooth surface, he picked out the missing hand. It gave it a weathered appearance of being old, damaged at some time in its history although he knew this one to be a copy. He read the word scratched into the back, *LEFT*.

"So, you're needed too tonight. The key to a clue maybe, so what with me, this paper and you, ushabti, we are the three keys to success... the treble clef you might say! That's what we shall be known as. *Treble Clef.*"

He spent a moment scribbling a few details on some headed notepaper that was lying on the desk and popped it into an envelope adding the name Mr David Hale. He slipped it into his pocket.

***

The evening was fine as he locked his bedroom door and descended into the lobby. It was quiet apart from the noise of a television behind a door marked *Private*. What he was about to experience was far more fun than anything they could tempt him with on the television and he felt a flush of excitement as the cool of the evening met him. He headed directly to the Mykonos restaurant. A waiter was setting some of the outside tables in readiness for the evening. He had a quiet word and handed over the envelope. The waiter nodded and tucked it into his jacket pocket.

"See you later!"

Within ten minutes Alan was walking up Victoria Avenue. He noticed the Harrogate Justice Centre and stopped to admire the building before continuing. The library was to his left. Approaching it, he noticed what looked like a bundle of rags piled against the short wall. Clothing hung from the railing as if it were a wardrobe. He then saw the paper cup just in front of the pile and he relaxed. He took a pound from his pocket and dropped it in. A grunt emanated from beneath the woollen cap as the concealed figure stirred.

There was nobody on the steps. Traffic moved freely and the occasional passer-by either smiled or ignored him.

"You'll need these. Put them on."

Alan felt himself jump as something touched his elbow and he turned defensively, a short sound emanating with his own breath. The bundle of blankets was now empty and the bearded figure, partially concealed beneath the woollen cap, faced him. What features he could see were wrinkled and dirt ingrained. In his open-fingered gloved hand was a pair of very dark wraparound sunglasses containing side pieces made up of darkened glass and some earphones.

"I've been asked to give you these and then this note. I can't read so don't ask me what it says. If you does as it says and lets me take you to where I've been told to, I'll get twenty quid, if not, I'm getting back in there. Thanks for the quid!" He pointed to his nest of blankets.

Alan read the note:

Earphones linked by Bluetooth to a phone in our homeless friend's pocket. Listen, as there are a couple of clues you'll need to remember mixed with the music.

He'll guide you, as you'll see bugger all once those glasses are on. If you fail to comply he's been told to stay just where he is. If you remove either at any time, the game ends. You wanted different… you've got different.

The Game Keeper.

Alan read the note again and felt the anxiety build in his stomach. This was silly. "Escape room I was told. None of this bollocks was mentioned."

The man looked at Alan and shrugged his shoulder before turning as if to climb back into the blankets.

"Okay, okay, in for a penny in for a pound." He took the headset and the dark glasses.

"Twenty quid more like it." He grasped hold of Alan's arm.

Everything went quiet and very dark, in fact, he could see nothing. Fingers lifted the earphone from his left ear and he spoke, "I'll guide you, it's not far, believe me." He then repositioned it. The theme from the film, 'The Great Escape' filled his head causing him to laugh. Suddenly he saw the funny side of it all and felt more at ease.

"It's theatrical, I'll give him that," Alan said under his breath.

***

Quinn had left and the next shift had been brought up to speed by April. The next day's briefing was planned for eight and that was early enough for a Sunday morning. Looking at the clock she stretched and wondered how Cyril and Owen had enjoyed their time away. Switching off the lights, she noticed that the hum continued. It was obviously ever-present. She savoured the responsibility her promotion had brought.

***

The street was quieter than it had been the night before but then it was still early for a Saturday. The occasional passers-by glanced at Valerie as she stood in the empty shop doorway. She had a scarf around her head and a cat travel basket at her feet. Those who noticed might assume she was obviously waiting for someone. It was then that she heard and saw the two men moving uncomfortably down the street. At first, because of their swaying motion she assumed them to be drunks. She moved out a little to get a better view before bending as if to look at the cat inside the basket.

Alan felt dizzy and a little nauseous. Being almost dragged the final part of the journey was more than a little disconcerting. Listening to the tune on a loop was beginning to annoy him. He had visualised Steve McQueen leaping over the barbed wire fence on the motorbike at least five times and on each occasion he saw the same result. They had now come to a stop. Even above the music he heard what sounded like a shutter of some kind being opened. He felt the tug at his elbow and he was moved forward a number of steps. His headphones were removed.

"Leave the glasses for the moment, please. Thank you." The voice was soft and unthreatening.

"Twenty pounds and very well done!"

Alan sensed the man who had brought him move away but not far. It was strange, he had not picked up a smell of body odour or bad breath and considering where he had seen him and his general appearance, that now seemed incongruous. The butterflies of nerves fluttered yet again within his stomach. The sudden sound of the falling shutter made him instinctively turn but still all was in darkness.

Valerie watched as the shutter was pulled down. Nobody left. She closed her eyes and visualised both men before quickly returning home. She would make notes of what she had witnessed and hopefully the confusion in her mind would clear.

"The game will begin in five minutes, Alan. When you're instructed to remove your glasses, you will see a small table illuminated by a single candle. Deposit anything you have brought with you, your phone, keys and any personal items into the box and close it. Lock it and keep the key with you for your own peace of mind. However, you will need the figure you were asked to bring and the note you received at the guesthouse. I take it you have both?"

"I do. That was clever but not too inventive." He specifically used the word *clever*.

"Yes, exactly. *Only the clever ever manages escape.* Once you've done that you'll see a door. Go through and you'll be in the first of three escape rooms. It will be dark but after three minutes the room will be lit. The time will begin then. May I thank you for taking part and may I say, as they do on the opening night in the theatre, *break a leg*."

Chapter Twenty-Four

D avid Hale had sent Alan three text messages during the course of the day but received no reply. It was when he was driving home that the text came through. Thinking it was Alan, he stopped the car.

David,

We met in the pub the other night in Harrogate. You said you were a keen gamer. I have a friend with the ultimate escape room. You get longer than an hour, but the stakes are higher too. Still interested? Let's say that you are. It's a game you will play alone against the clock. If you win, not only will you be rewarded in knowing that you may well be the first, but also there is a much more interesting prize at stake… This is only offered to a select few. I'll send you another message on Sunday to let you know the finer mechanics of our game. Do not tell your mate, as we will select only one of you.

He reread it. "Is that where you are? You scheming bugger." Suddenly he was filled with excitement. He had thought the man who had befriended them in the pub was just talk, but he then remembered the ushabti figure. "That's why you asked me for it before your day off. You're there playing. You poker-faced bastard."

***

"When you enter the room it will be dark. After a few seconds the lights will come on and your time will begin. If, for whatever reason you feel beaten, all you need to do is stand still and raise your left hand. I say again, left hand." He emphasised the instruction. "That will be your humiliating signal of capitulation.

There are cameras in each of the rooms. However, no help can or will be offered, as the impressive prize for the first successful escapee has to be truly earned. Do you understand? Raise your right hand if you do."

The voice echoed through what appeared to be vintage speakers.

Alan raised his hand.

"Good. I'm glad you didn't raise your left as one player did, or should I now call you all inmates? Yes, inmates. Well, one inmate raised the wrong hand at this early stage with dire consequences... He failed immediately."

Alan heard the familiar click of an electronic lock opening. He moved into the room and closed the door. It was in total darkness. Slowly the lights grew until a faint yellow ambience filled the room. The lights were trapped behind angled metal frames; covered inserts of wired security glass finished the fitting. They were positioned like coving between the wall and the ceiling. The door he had come through now closed and locked, resembling part of the wall and a traditional cell door was to his right. A large combination lock was attached to the wrought iron hasp and staple. The room was a perfect prison cell. It made Alan smile. "This is bloody good," he said out loud, unsure as to whether he could be heard.

"Glad you like it, Alan. Good luck."

The walls did have ears and he made a mental note to be more careful in what he said. He knew that the first thing he must do was to memorise the position of the objects within the room. Experience had taught him he must move nothing, as the layout of the objects might well be a clue or a partial clue. In the past he had moved books and then found each had contained a number for the combination. By carelessly rearranging them he had lost the sequence. Looking now at the books on the shelf he noted their titles but found nothing of significance. Taking each, he checked for any insert before replacing them onto the shelf. It was then he heard the tapping, as if travelling along one of the pipes that were positioned along the edge of the ceiling. He smiled and used his fingernail to make a mark on the dusty floor. He had seen this done before but it played constantly and annoyingly on a loop. He waited for a pause knowing the sequence would begin again.

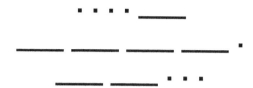

It then stopped. He waited but all was silent. 4, 9 and 7. He had the first three numbers. He knew little Morse code other that S.O.S but he had memorised the numbers after playing a game in Belgium.

"Very clever of you to pick up on that. Listening is a key skill. Some players don't have a clue." The voice again appeared to come from some hidden, old loudspeaker. "Sorry to interrupt."

***

She had just walked and fed Ralph, her adopted Great Dane when the call came. April stirred what was the start of a bolognese sauce. It was a call April did not want to receive.

"Hi Dan. All okay?"

"We have an eighty-five per cent positive ID on facial recognition for Drakes at the Games Convention and it also places him on Parliament Street at about the same time Carruthers and his group were last seen. That's not all. We've also run tests on Tommy Boardman after receiving an image sent from his employer or should I say previous employer. Apparently, he left immediately after the incident with Drakes but that's a story for a little later. Amazingly, Colin Boardman was also at the convention, the man who supposedly threw

Carruthers out for playing games. He's also still in Harrogate. We checked the town's CCTV and he was seen and identified on four occasions by these specialists *Flash* employed. There are other times he might have been seen but owing to the film quality they can't be certain."

"Do we have an address?"

"Only for Drakes. Cleared with upstairs and officers are on their way. I suggested they be armed but the powers that be said not at this stage. Warrant requested and should be with us quickly. With it being a murder enquiry it doesn't need to go through all the hoops. Forensics team too is standing by to search."

"Shit!" April exclaimed as the sauce began to boil frantically. The smell told her it was in the process of burning and sticking to the bottom of the pan whilst also beginning to smoke. "Bloody hell, Dan!" Ralph simply turned, yawned and curled his long limbs as best he could. She quickly moved the pan and turned off the cooker. "I'm turning into a man, Dan, can only seem to do one thing at a time these days." It was then the smoke alarm added to the chaos.

His laughter down the phone lifted her mood.

"Not at all funny, well not where I'm standing. So what's this information on Boardman?"

"You recall Drakes was supposedly compensated as he was thought to have suffered a severe good hiding at the hands of the anti-hunt campaigners when he was out beating for the shoot? Well, that may have been the case. We now know that both he and Tommy Boardman found employment elsewhere in the same capacity. According to this information, Drakes had suggested that their boss, the landowner, a Lord Craimer, had been involved in some deviant sexual practices with person or persons employed on the estate. Drakes had discussed this with Boardman and supposedly shown him explicit images of the alleged acts. It was suggested that Drakes tried some form of blackmail and consequently received a bloody good hiding and that included suffering some gunshot wounds. I believe the photographs were retrieved and Drakes sent down the road with some financial compensation to keep it quiet. Why Tommy Boardman left shortly afterwards I can't say. Strangely, we now see Tommy's brother and Drakes possibly in league. There's nothing further on Tommy. He's been located and will be questioned in due course but again we're doing nothing to frighten off Drakes."

"Is this all speculation or do you have evidence?"

"All rumour but information from a good source who was there and who knows more than he's telling. That source, April, is our friend, Richard Carruthers. I had a drive over and politely suggested how much I could disrupt his precious timetable by insisting he came over to Harrogate for questioning as frequently as we requested. It was then the floodgates opened. I have it all recorded."

"Worth burning my dinner for that, Dan. Well done, you."

Chapter Twenty-Five

Alan had lifted the one sheet from the bed but there was nothing underneath. He checked the graffiti along each wall and then the pin-ups and posters. It was more of a challenge than he had anticipated. He had left his watch locked in the box outside along with his other personal items and so he had no concept of time.

"I can see that you're on a roll, Alan. You've had twenty-six minutes."

Alan continued to check the graffiti on the walls as methodically as he could, considering the light quality. As he came to the final wall he noticed the toilet roll standing on the floor next to the toilet. "...You're on a roll!" He picked up the toilet roll. It felt more like tracing paper than what he was used to. Unrolling it, he counted the attached sheets. He had got to five when the piece came away; obviously it had been torn previously and rerolled. He continued and only one sheet came away. He had his five numbers.

Fumbling with the lock he knew that there were two options, either the initial three numbers or last. He decided on the latter course of action. He added the numbers five, one, four, nine and seven to the tumblers and as the last one rolled into position the lock sprang open. Quickly he flicked off the lock and the hasp from the staple and swung open the door. Although it gave the impression of being made of iron it swung with ease. It brought a smile to Alan's face.

As the door closed behind him the lights along the skirting boards illuminated the old green linoleum flooring. He laughed out loud. "The old green mile. Stephen King would be proud."

The room, being narrow and but a few strides long, looked more like a very short corridor; a mile it was not and could never be said to be. He stretched out both arms and easily touched the sides. Immediately he saw the two doors, one either side a few metres away. There was no graffiti on the walls that he could see although the light here was also poor. It was then he saw the torch on the floor in a far corner. Cautious initially, he ensured he knew its exact location before picking it up. He also noticed one door required a key whilst the other did not seem to have a lock at all. However, it did have a triangular yellow sign saying, DANGER OF DEATH, and a symbol showing a lightning bolt striking a falling figure. He frowned.

***

The police car pulled up next to chalet 4 and two officers looked round. There appeared to be no movement. It was not yet fully dark so there were no lights on. An officer looked through the windows and tried the two doors as the other stood back monitoring the procedure.

"He's not been in all day… not since early doors as far as I know!" a man shouted from a few feet away.

The officer trying the door jumped.

"Sorry, didn't mean to startle you. He left very early this morning. Car picked him up on the road, yonder." He waved a hand in the vague direction. "Tends to be out most weekdays and occasionally at the weekends but not always."

"Do you know where?"

"Probably work." He shrugged his shoulders as if he neither knew nor cared. "Sees all, hears all and says nowt our Gary."

"What kind of car?"

The man, dressed in a pair of tracksuit bottoms and a vest, simply raised his shoulders again. "It was black or grey, could've even been dark blue. Couldn't really say. Why, what's he done?"

Ignoring the question, the officer asked his name. "What time does he normally get back, Mark, when he's been out since early doors?"

"Not late usually but there's been the odd occasion when it's the early hours of the morning. As I said, keeps himself to himself. Not a bad neighbour. Now you're going to tell me he's a mass bloody murderer." He laughed.

The officer laughed too, thanked him and returned to the car to call in the information.

Dan Grimshaw cursed under his breath. He really did not want to go in all guns blazing, crashing through the front door, blue lights and sirens flashing and screaming, not at this stage and certainly not considering there were holidaymakers close by. He called control to patch him through to the police officers in the car.

"See if anyone's got a key. I want the place searching. I don't mean touch anything, just the once over. We have a warrant on the way. Try a neighbour and then the site manager. You've got their emergency number so use it for goodness sake. Call back to me personally when you've finished."

***

Alan inspected the torch and immediately registered that the door marked with the warning sign and the torch were both linked to electricity and power, albeit in different forms.

"Maybe that's the way out. No key, but the torch may be the key." He leaned over to take hold of the handle but just before he could touch it a bolt of static electricity jumped the short distance. "Shit!" He had made a wrong call. He suddenly heard the sound of a bell chiming slowly but methodically as if counting down the time.

"A division bell. You have it all."

"Clever. Not the real sounding ring of that within Parliament but the one taken from the Pink Floyd album, you'll note. For the first time you're now under the clock. You've got

174

eight minutes to make your decision. It's about choice, as someone said, it's about the yea and the nay... which door will you choose? One is the correct choice and the other..." there was a pause... "A failure. Simple as that."

The bell continued to sound.

The torch was unusual in shape, a bulbous light source with a knobbly rubber element to one end. He pressed it and immediately light was emitted from the numerous small LED bulbs. Alan knew immediately what this would do. "Black light... a valuable piece of kit for every CSI," he mumbled to himself as he shone it first on the wall facing him. There was nothing visible but as he turned to the right-side wall, immediately illuminated was a list of neatly written words. They were in an ink invisible to the naked eye but glowed clearly once lit with UV:

RAZOR, ASP, BATTLESHIP, ACCUBATION, UNLOVED.

"Considering where you are, my friend, what word comes next?" The voice from the speaker questioned.

Alan kept the light source on the writing that glowed green and was now highly visible. This type of script did not help its legibility and the fact each letter was written in capitals also proved confusing. He read each one paying particular attention to the letter placement within each word; he had seen something like this before and once the sequence was identified there was usually an option of four words to choose from but on this occasion the word had then to be guessed. The audible volume of the bell's chime was gradually growing weaker.

"The Green Mile is the walk to the death chamber so... The first word begins with R, the next word, second letter S so in the third word, the following letter should be T... Got you! The word I need has a sixth letter of W. A type of execution... Gallows. It's gallows!"

Immediately the bell stopped, the room was flooded with light and from beneath the door marked *DANGER OF DEATH* appeared an envelope.

***

Dan Grimshaw tapped the desk with his fingers as his right hand squeezed a soft rubber ball the physiotherapist had recommended to strengthen his wrists. He worked each hand in turn until the ache proved too much. It was the waiting that was always the worst. It was then the phone rang.

"Yes, anything?"

"We've been through the place but disturbed nothing as instructed. All I can report is that it hasn't been used to any form of TLC but it's also not exactly in the category of shit hole. Let's say it's in the running for coming a close second. There's no firearm cabinet, nor did we see any ammunition, and for a gamekeeper, this surprised us, unless he keeps all the tools of his trade with his employer. As instructed, we've not rooted, just casually looked around. What he does have is quite a collection of stuffed animals, typically English game and fish. Some, however, have seen better days, especially those without display cases."

"Games? Figures? Did you see anything to link him with these gaming groups?"

"There's a figure, strange bloody thing with what looks like elephants' trunks or maybe octopus tentacles sprouting from its head. It has bat's wings and the general appearance of a lizard. It's not very big and it's on a shelf over the fireplace."

Grimshaw stood up and looked at a photograph on the noticeboards which had been taken in Carruthers's garage. It was just as described. "It's Cthulhu, some imaginary figure, it seems to be a common denominator with some of the key players in this case. Photograph it and forward me the image. Wait there and when our friend Drakes returns, caution him and request that he accompanies you back to the station."

"And if…" He did not get time to finish.
"Arrest him."

***

Alan picked up the envelope. It was sealed.

Congratulations.
Nobody has managed to get this far without showing some weaknesses and all but failing. You've been magnificent. Last clue for this, the penultimate room, is now yours. And after the green mile comes…?
Good Luck!

It had clearly been written by the same hand that had penned the puzzle on the wall. Taking care in opening the envelope, Alan withdrew a card. The bell started to chime again but this time much more weakly than before. It was amazing how the sounds amplified the anxiety level. Alan had to admit that he had never experienced a game like this one. It was certainly cleverly thought out and wonderfully executed. He laughed as he considered his choice of word… *executed*. His mind drifted momentarily, wondering what the cost of such an experience would eventually be to the average punter, but then suddenly remembered the bell.

On the card was a series of numbers:

? 34 21 13 8 5 ?
Simple?

Alan put a finger across his lips as he quickly scanned the numbers. "Fifty-five and three!" he called out as loudly as possible. His sheer joy was clearly evident. The bell stopped. Alan followed by shouting out a resounding, "Yes!"

"Well done, Alan. The yeas have it!"

The door to the right with the warning sign sprang open. Alan left the Green Mile behind as he stepped through to be greeted by the smallest of the three rooms he had been in. He knew that he was close to the end, close to escaping and he bubbled with anticipation.

Chapter Twenty-Six

Tommy Boardman sat in interview room two. April and Brian faced him. Both had been surprised that he had volunteered to come in after their initial call, particularly on a Saturday evening. He was older than Colin, his brother, and it was clear from his skin colour and from his hands that he had spent much of his life out-of-doors. He had removed his well-worn flat cap before entering and that sat cradled in his ever-moving hands. A metal badge announced he was part of some fishing society, and others depicted birds in fine, colourful enamel.

"Thank you for coming in on a Saturday evening, Mr Boardman."

"Just another day to us country folk, people with lots to do at this time of the year and who don't have time to bugger about. I believe this is to do with Drakes and I'm happy to assist in any way I can."

"What do you know about Mr Drakes?"

Tommy slipped a pocket watch from his jacket. "How long you got?"

Brian glanced at April and realised the error in his questioning. "Yes, sorry, that was a bit open."

"Look, to kick off, let me say I've known Gary Drakes for a bloody long time. He worked for me when I was Head Keeper up in Scotland. He's a simple man if you get my drift, back of the queue when they were handing out brains, like. We said he was thick. Bloody good at his job though and would never refuse to do owt. Brave lad too. Could hold his own in the pub. Seen him try to drop a few big 'uns who got too cocky, but often ended up the worse for such encounters."

"So why did he leave?" April asked.

"Laird we were working for was a bit of a bully, also liked to…" he paused, looking at April and then back at Brian, "…push his advances on the weaker employees and I don't mean the weaker sex here, Miss, they were of no interest to him. He was married too. I mean anyone he could bully and coerce, if that's the right word. Young lads would suddenly be promoted or find themselves with a pay rise if you get my drift. Well, Drakes saw all of this and as I said, couldn't just turn a blind eye. We told him to leave it. Any road, one day he came to me with some pictures, Polaroid jobs and not too clear either but you could just make them out. Showed the Laird in situations he wouldn't like the papers or his wife to see."

"So, Drakes blackmailed him?"

Tommy shook his head. "Not that bright. He just wanted what he thought was justice for the lads. Unbeknown to me he put one of these pictures in an envelope and came to me with it. It was sealed and he asked me to write the Laird's name on it and leave it on his desk. It was the Laird's birthday that week and I thought it was a card. Said it was important and to make sure he got it. So I did. I honestly didn't know what was in it or it wouldn't have got further than the fire in the entrance hall."

"So, when did you know what was in it?"

"When the boss sent for me. He held up the envelope and smiled. *Your writing, Tommy?* he asked and I nodded. He then said, *Drakes?* Thinking it was still a birthday greeting I said aye and smiled. He said, and I kid you not, *I must thank him personally in some small way that he'll remember for a while.*"

"So, you thought nothing more about it?"

"I thought it was a good move for a lad who had no brains. I thought he was in for a tip. It was afterwards I realised what was in the envelope and that everyone knew Drakes had this camera. He'd shown it around enough times and taken pictures when we were out on shoots. Anyway, I discovered he'd got someone to write on the back, *If working like this can get a pay rise, we should get one for not seeing it,* or something like that. The exact wording I can't recall."

"So, what happened?"

"That week was the shoot so it wasn't the best of times to do anything like that, let alone with the boss. The big house was full of guests, bloody important ones who were paying top dollar, thousands. It went on for a few weeks, that's where the main money is made for the estate. The tips too for the boys and girls were bloody good. Anyway, we had a bit of trouble with the anti-hunt brigade, always do. They can be a hard shower of bastards believe me, and you people don't help that much. There were a few confrontations, nothing too bloody as some of our lads are brought in specially to deal with it. They're the ones who wouldn't know one end of a woodcock from the other but that's not why they were there."

"What about Drakes?"

"I'm coming to that. Drakes was beating to the west of the estate, driving the birds over the guns. Anyway, he goes AWOL but that can happen when we close for the end of the day. Some miss the transport back. Trouble was, he didn't show the next day either so I went to where he should have been and found some of his belongings. It was then I heard a shot and out of the woods came Drakes. Someone had given him a right hiding. He'd been shot in the hand too. It wasn't that bad, a bit peppered. It was then I saw the Laird and one of the paid lads. Drakes just looked at me and said, *Sorry!* He dropped at my feet. What was strange and what struck me as odd, steam was rising from his head, he'd obviously been running.

"The Laird stopped some distance away. *That stinking, snivelling piece of shit tried to blackmail me, me! I'm the man who gave the underhand worm a bloody job when he didn't have the brains to be employed elsewhere and this is how he tried to repay me. He's bloody lucky he's not buried in the peat and he's fortunate that he found you, otherwise who knows what this morning might have brought.* I told him that Drakes had suffered enough and needed a hospital, but the laird just said that he was getting no hospital but would receive treatment back at the house. At least Drakes was with me and I knew he was safe for the time being."

***

It was the chair that attracted Alan's attention. Again, time and effort had gone into creating an authentic-looking electric chair. Behind it was a mirror set into the wall and to the right a narrow door. Along the left-hand wall ran a shelf on which were positioned a row of small figures. Each one was different and each perfectly painted. On closer inspection there was a gap. Alan realised why. Taking the ushabti figure from his pocket he placed it on the shelf.

Walking around the back of the chair Alan observed all the straps and buckles. They should provide a clue. The combination lock required four numbers. From behind the mirror two people watched carefully. The inmate had performed much better than they had ever expected.

"He could do this."

"It's this one that will take some thinking. When we put the countdown on the speaker he'll panic. Watch, Christ, I would."

Alan sat on the electric chair and allowed his eyes to scan every metre of the walls. It was then the tick of the clock began.

"One hundred, ninety-nine, ninety-eight…"

He moved back to the shelf and took hold of the ushabti turning it quickly and looking at the back. He read the letters L, E F, and T. "Each has a value in the alphabet. E is five, F, six so L is… twelve and T is worth twenty, so that's twelve, five, six and twenty. The first and last both have a two, two positives make a negative… take those away…"

"Fifty-five, fifty-four…"

"So, that's one, five, six and zero." He added them to the combination lock… Nothing!

"Thirty-two, thirty-one…"

Alan quickly reversed the sequence starting with zero and he was rewarded by the sound of the lock springing open. The countdown stopped at *nineteen* and it was replaced by the theme tune to "The Great Escape". He pulled open the door to be greeted by a brick wall. His heart sank.

Chapter Twenty-Seven

"So, what happened when you got Drakes back to the house?"

"One of the guests was a doctor and let's say, he was a very close friend of the Laird if you get my meaning. He patched him up and I was told to take him to his cottage and then return. On reaching the cottage it had been completely turned over, furniture slashed, drawers emptied. Nothing was left intact. What we did find was ash in the fireplace and a broken camera. They'd found the other pictures and burned them. I got him as comfortable as possible and then went back as per instructions. I was given an envelope, a big one."

"For you?" Brian asked.

Tommy laughed. "I was informed that Drakes would be off the estate within twenty-four hours and if he were, then what was in the envelope was his on the understanding it would be enough to keep his mouth shut."

There was a pause. Tommy kept screwing up his cap and then releasing it as if he were replaying the final moments over and over.

"That's it? So, what did he do?"

Tommy looked back at both officers in turn. "So he left. What would you have done?"

"Where did he go?"

"I have a brother, as you know, who lives in Richmond. I suppose we are brothers but... Anyway, I knew Drakes was fragile so I asked Colin if he could stay with him and his wife. They lived in a flat attached to his parents-in-law's place. He'd pay his way but he needed a bit of support whilst we sorted out something permanent for him in the way of work and a place to live. He went there. Colin's wife took a shine to him. He helped with the garden and brought in fresh rabbit and the odd game. She liked that. He'd prepare it for them too."

"And you?"

"I got my marching orders and in place of a bung I was given excellent references and a couple of months' salary. One of his new boys got my job but to be fair the Laird introduced me to my boss and I almost walked straight into the position. Managed to get Drakes in about six months later. At first he was only temporary but then he filled a role similar to the one he had before. He also got the lodge and before you ask, you can guess how that was paid for."

***

The car pulled up at the end of the driveway to the campsite. The two officers watched as the figure walked past the Reception building. On seeing the police car he paused.

"Mr Drakes?" The officer approached.

Drakes stood. He held a small petrol chainsaw in one hand and it hung to his side. "And you are?"

"PC Livesey. I need to ask you to come with me to the station. You're not under arrest at this moment but I still have to caution you."

The other officer approached.

"Come to the station about what? Look, I've had a long, hard bloody day. I'm hungry, filthy and I need a piss."

"We have time. Grab a shower and something to eat but make it quick."

Drakes stashed the chainsaw in a metal cabinet that appeared bolted to the side of the lodge and entered. The officers looked at each other. "We missed that!"

They heard the shower run and one sat by the door whilst the other waited in the car ensuring Drakes would not escape through a window. Drakes rang Tommy.

The ringtone was that of a traditional phone and he stopped talking.

"Answer it, please," said April. "We could all use a coffee. Sugar?"

Tommy nodded. It showed it was Drakes. "Hi. Where are you?" He listened to Drakes ramble on. He put the phone on speaker. "You're on speaker. I'm at Harrogate cop shop talking about you. If they want you here, come. Let's get whatever they want sorted out. The last thing you need is to lose your job and if you've done nothing wrong then there's nothing to worry about."

***

The door he had come through to enter the execution room opened and the noise startled Alan, but not as much as the pop of the champagne cork leaving the bottle and crashing against the ceiling. Alan looked at the man holding the bottle. It was the same man who had given him the ushabti figure in the pub. He bowed to Alan. "Bravo, young man. I have to say you left us breathless. Your secular knowledge is most impressive." He handed the bottle to Alan, left the room and returned with three glasses and a small silver trophy on a tray. Taking the bottle, he filled the trophy first and then the glasses.

"Now, before we celebrate your escape, I want to introduce you to the man who created it all, designed the sets, painted them and devised the way you were brought here. Jim, please come in."

Jim West entered the room. There was little space for the three of them. It was Jim who spoke.

"Please sit, Alan. This man you see before you was the tramp who brought you here, as well as the chap who discovered you in the pub. We met in the theatre and he's helping me out and having some fun. Alan, meet Stan."

The glasses were filled and both men lifted theirs. "Our heartfelt congratulations. We hope that you not only found it challenging but also enjoyable and we would love you to review our unique, individual escape room when you've had time to reflect fully on the experience. Cheers."

Alan first drank the small amount from the trophy and then was handed his glass. They chatted for about thirty minutes. Alan was handed another bottle and he drank a further two glasses.

"I was more thirsty than I thought and the bubbles have gone straight to my head."

Jim brought in the locked box containing Alan's personal items. Slipping on his watch he noticed that he had been in the rooms for nearly two hours. It was 9.12. "Sorry, gents, must fly. I don't wish to be rude but you said something about a reward worth winning?"

Jim removed his wallet and took out five twenty-pound notes. "Well done, but please, a review would help us."

Stan took him back to the front room and raised the shutter. It was then Alan noticed the equipment. "Another room in the planning?"

"Maybe," Stan answered. "Thanks for taking part. Don't forget to give your mate this." He handed him the ushabti figure. "I've already sent him a challenge. I haven't mentioned you as yet and I'd be grateful if you can keep your stunning escape a secret for forty-eight hours. Is that okay?"

"That'll be harder than the game… I can't promise but I'll do my best."

***

Jim was clearing away the glasses. He checked his phone and saw he had three missed calls from Valerie. He dialled her number.

"Thank goodness, Jim. What's going on at that place of yours? I saw a tramp leading a young man inside and then the shutter came down. The lad was wearing dark glasses. They both seemed drunk to me. I was worried for you."

"Valerie, Valerie. They were simply sampling the new escape room. One was an actor friend of mine, he was the tramp and the young fellow was an expert in these matters. Because we neither wanted him to see the façade of the place nor know where it is until we open. We had to create that charade, besides I think it made it a tad more theatrical. We went about creating the whole thing before he arrived. He thought it was a wonderful experience and he's going to review it. We may well have a new and successful venture on our hands."

Valerie answered with one word. "We?"

***

Alan realised he was unsure of his way and removed his mobile phone but it was dead. He pressed the *on* button but nothing appeared on screen. "Bloody battery!" He suddenly felt very light headed and nauseous. He staggered and put a hand against the wall. His fingers tingled and his vision began to blur. "I need to get home."

Chapter Twenty-Eight

D rakes looked at Tommy who smiled and gave him a hug. "You're alright, mate, they know the history. They want to know about Colin Boardman. Be truthful and hide nothing. I'll be here. If you want a solicitor we can have one too. I've nothing to hide as I've done nothing wrong and I hope neither have you."

"Other than the pictures, and then I wanted only what was right. I didn't want anything other than what was due to me and a few quid more for the other lads. You believe me don't you, Tommy?"

Tommy rested a hand on his shoulder. "You'll be fine."

April noted the statement matched Tommy's until the section where he went missing.

"I left the three other beaters to go for a piss. It was cold. Any road, I don't remember much until I woke up in the old sheep shelter, you know the one, Tommy, by the narrow burn? I've not told you this till now, Tommy, I was too ashamed. Anyway, I woke up with a cracking headache and my trousers and long johns round by my gaiters and boots. I didn't know what hurt more my head or my arse. He told me that if I ever tried to spread those rumours again it would be a red-hot piece of steel and that'd give me something to moan about. He'd raped me, Tommy, the bastard raped me."

Drakes struggled to finish the sentence before breaking down. His shoulders heaved and released a wail not dissimilar to that of an injured animal. Tommy moved across immediately, wrapping an arm around his shoulder and drew him closer.

"Shhh! It's okay, we understand."

"I've tried to forget it, but it eats, Tommy, it's like cancer. I feel so unclean. Some days I want to just…"

April rose and went to get a cup of water. She knew right now he could do with something a lot stronger but that was impossible. She had seen a number of men cry during interviews, many searching for sympathy, but this was born from guilt, fear and frustration built up over the years and months. She could have wept for him.

He sipped the water, wiping his tears on the sleeve of his jacket; the trickle of snot that ran from his left nostril to his lip was also removed in the same movement. "I'm so sorry. When I realised what had happened, I managed to pull up my pants and I ran at him. I'd have killed him, as God is my witness, Tommy, I'd have murdered the bastard and that's when the big bastard with him gave me a right seeing to. The Laird just laughed and then he stopped him."

"What about the shooting?" April asked. Her voice lowered in sympathy.

"I don't know how long I was there. It was dark when I came to after the beating, and light when I saw the chance to get away. They were at the far end of the pen, probably planning what to do with me. I remembered the Laird was drinking from a silver flask and laughing. I just legged it. It was then I felt the pellets spray my hand as I got to the trees. Not long after that, maybe within minutes, I saw you."

April looked across at Brian Smirthwaite and raised her eyebrows. Sexual assault cases involving the high, the mighty and the famous were growing in number and becoming an ever-increasing burden on police resources and at this time, it was probably the last thing they needed to hear. April switched off the tape. "Are you okay to continue, Mr Drakes?"

Drakes nodded. "That was the worst bit. I don't like going over that and… I've never talked about it, not proud, just so ashamed, so never told anyone in public, like and in front of a lady too… it just wasn't easy, I'm sorry, but I want you to know I'm not like that."

Tommy put his hand on Drakes's shoulder again. "We know that. We go back a long way and I consider you to be an honest man. Well done for speaking up. That's what they anticipated you would be, ashamed and full of guilt to the point of being dumb. They wanted you to be embarrassed enough to keep your mouth shut. It's a game to them. It's their way of keeping their activities hidden from view. They rule by fear and intimidation and money, of course."

Most of those words meant little to Drakes, who sipped the water.

"So, when you came to Richmond, Tommy's brother, Colin, let you stay with them?"

"Felicity was really kind. Made me feel special. I tended the garden when I wasn't working and did a bit of maintenance about the place. Even helped her mum when she needed it, nothing major, painting, window cleaning, just general stuff. The old lady, Felicity's mum, even taught me to knit."

For the first time since the start of the interview April saw the glimmer of a smile and some happiness in his eyes. She realised what a simple man he really was.

"Did you ever meet Felicity's father?" Brian asked.

Drakes shook his head. "Dead before my time. Tommy will know more." He turned to look at his friend.

"I'm not that sure I can tell you anything. Christ, can't really recall much about my own parents let alone hers. Think I only met her a handful of times."

"Was Colin supportive of all the things you did, Mr Drakes?"

"He let me stay as a favour to Tommy but he was fine. I think he was a bit jealous like. Felicity always brought me tea and biscuits when I was working in the garden or jobbing. I was grateful they'd offered me a roof when I needed it and that's why I returned the favour when he asked me to help Kevin. I put the lad up who had rented their flat. When her mum died…"

April stopped him. "We're aware of that and how Kevin Carruthers rented their old flat. Why did he ask you?"

"He said that things were a bit complicated and Colin wanted him out of the house. He really said needed, and not wanted, and he would be grateful if I could return the favour. I couldn't really say no, I wouldn't say no." There was a long pause. "Bit of a weird bugger he was though!"

It was Brian's turn to ask and from the way he approached the question April knew it was going to upset both Tommy and Drakes. "Did you or did Felicity ever make sexual advances to one another?"

There was silence.

***

The traffic noises seemed amplified and the scream of a police car, all blue flashing lights and noise, appeared closer than it was but it brought Alan to his senses.

"Are you alright?" A hand gently gripped Alan's elbow. "You look a little unsteady young man."

"I feel dreadful. I'm trying to find my B&B but I can't even recall its name, a whisky comes to mind but…"

"*Grants*?"

"That's it, yes. Thanks. Is it far?"

"No, it's just a short walk. Ten minutes at the most. I can give you directions or I can escort you. Either way's no bother."

The illuminated sign soon came into view. "It's just here."

"Thank you so much. I'd never have found it. Can I give you some money for your help?"

"Not at all. It's my random act of kindness for the day. Think nothing of it. Do you need me to help you with the key?"

"No, I'm fine. Thank you."

The front door was still open as it was not yet ten. He fumbled in his pocket until he found the keys. Turning he saw his escort watching from the gate. He raised his thumb. Alan responded and opened the inner door. "Thank you. Good night." For some reason he whispered the words and his shepherd moved off.

The television was still on in the room marked *Private.* The drone of the indecipherable voices suddenly seemed reassuring and he felt comfortable. Within minutes he had drunk two glasses of water, taken two paracetamol and was in bed. Even though his head swirled and his fingers and toes felt numb, he was pleased with his evening's work.

***

Drakes looked at Tommy who nodded. "Tell what you have to tell. Nobody's judging you."

"It was her, she came to me once when I was in the garden. She'd brought lemonade. I'd been digging. She asked me to show her what I'd been preparing in the shed. I'd just sorted the cuttings and the seedlings and... It was just that once." He looked at each person in the room. The same fear had returned to his expression, as if the incriminations of the misdemeanour would damn him forever.

"Did her husband know, find out or suspect?" Brian asked. Realising he had provided maybe too many options he rephrased the question. "Did she tell her husband?"

"I don't think so. When we came out of the shed I saw her mother watching us from her bedroom window. Felicity didn't see her."

"Did she witness what went on or did she just see you enter and leave the shed?"

"Just go in and come out."

"How long were you in there?"

"Fifteen minutes, no more."

"Had you gone in there before with Mrs Boardman, Mr Drakes?"

"Yes, but not for that."

"Did you call her Felicity or Fliss?"

"Felicity, always. She wanted me to call her Fliss, especially after we did... any road, I couldn't, even more so after that. I knew then I'd have to find another place. I couldn't do that to someone who'd opened his door for me."

"Thank you, Mr Drakes, you've been very co-operative. I'll get one of the officers to run you home."

"If you've done with me too, I'll run him. It's what mates do."

Drakes looked at Tommy. "Sorry, Tommy."

"Mr Drakes, an officer noticed a model of this creature on your mantelpiece. May I ask why you have it?" He showed Drakes a photograph of the figure.

"Present from Kevin when he left, a thank you, like. He said it would keep me from harm and protect me."

"Thank you."

"Why were you at the Harrogate Games Convention? Do you play these sorts of games?"

For the second time Gary Drakes flushed. He turned quickly to Tommy and then back to Brian, clasping his hands until his knuckles showed white.

"I was meeting Kevin. He asked me to call on him if I was near Harrogate, that day. I thought I'd kill two birds with one stone, like. Met him and a mate of his. Can't remember his name. Had a pint with them too, up by the memory thing…"

"The Cenotaph?"

"Aye. They were going on to play some game or other so I said I was going home."

"Did you see either again that night?"

Drakes just shook his head.

"We need a yes or no answer, Mr Drakes."

"Sorry, no."

"Thank you both for your co-operation. We'll be in touch."

The two left. It was like a father leading home his son.

Brian looked at April. "Kill two birds with one stone, an unfortunate expression to use if I may say so."

April simply laughed and shook her head. "He's daft but not that daft. What a sad case." She picked up the cup from which Drakes had been drinking. "Get that checked immediately for DNA. Insist on RapidHIT."

Brian looked at her. One minute she was almost crying with him and then the next she was as cold as steel. He would never understand women, he thought.

"I need to talk to *Flash* and I need to do it now. Be prepared for an early kick-off tomorrow as a few more worms have appeared from what we'd hoped was an empty can."

Chapter Twenty-Nine

Cyril had not long parked the car and was about to call at *The Coach* for a swift half before bed. The ginnel linking Robert Street with West Park Road was dark and a solitary figure stood to one side. Cyril saw the red glow of a cigarette end before smelling the sweetness of the smoke that lingered like guilt. He would have loved to have stopped and had words but he was neither in the mood nor prepared to commit the time. His phone rang. He left it in his pocket until he emerged into the well-lit road. April's number was displayed.

"Bennett."

"Sorry to bother you, sir. Are you back or still at your mum's?"

"Just about to have a nightcap in the pub and then bed. What's up?"

April explained what had happened regarding the interview with Drakes and his time with the Boardmans. "So we have a case of historical rape to consider and you want to suggest to me that there might have been a murder committed by either Colin or Felicity Boardman?" He paused before entering the pub. "Briefing at eight in the morning. I want you and Brian with me at seven. Organise a car for me at six-thirty. It never seems to rain but pour."

***

The light to *Grant's* B&B sign was still illuminated at 2.30 in the morning. Harrogate had been busy but then it always was when the weather was fine. The wait had not been too bad and he had managed to snatch some sleep. This visit tonight was really a first for him, it was indulgent, for his entertainment and pleasure, not for revenge. It was now a game to determine how long he could play and to see if those who found the clues could stop him.

Holding the three keys in the palm of his hand he thought of his victim, remembering the look on Alan's face as he had solved the final clue. He had been successful after all and that was more than could be said for the other two losers. He sat back in the car seat as he recalled the moment his suspicions had been confirmed. It was when he saw Felicity leaving the flat, he realised then what was going on with Kevin. He had only returned home for his wallet, having left it on the kitchen table. There they both were, at it behind his back. That was the first time but there had been many more occasions and their meetings were becoming more frequent. When he encountered them, their eyes laughed as they turned to look at each other. Meeting Kevin's friend, John, with the swanky name, Van de Meer, Colin had been introduced as Fliss's husband, as if he were a nonentity, an appendage. He saw their amusement, felt it and it hurt. That had been the final straw, the gauntlet had been dropped.

Moving to Harrogate and renting Jim West's flat above the redundant shop had been the catalyst, the spark of the idea. It was as if they had come to him and said here are the mechanics of your new and murderous game of revenge. Jim West was so up his theatrical arse that he never stopped to think. Providing his stage settings were successful he was happy. Stan, just an amateur actor, always thought he had missed the boat that led to stardom. He had a pointless life, no wife, retirement and nothing only bit parts and games nights to keep himself amused; of course if you did not count painting little people.

He talked out loud to himself as if to crystallise his thoughts. "And as for Drakes? What plans for the poor, sad and dim-witted, Drakes?"

How her mother had gloated at the fact that Felicity and he enjoyed dibbing and potting. He remembered those were her very words, *dibbing and potting in the shed. Has Felicity been using Drakes's dibber today, Colin? According to my daughter, Drakes can use his dibber far better than you ever could.* He pulled down the sunshade and looked in the illuminated mirror.

"The old witch knew how far to go. It was not what she said but the manner in which she delivered her barbed comments. Still, everything comes to those who wait. Best served cold I think they recommend. Are we now ready?"

Opening the bag that was positioned on the passenger seat he observed the sheath in which three shards of cranberry glass were individually wrapped. There was a blue faience-like figure enveloped in plastic, a polythene bag, a small bottle and a large electrical tie.

It took three minutes from opening the gate to mounting the stairs to number 4. All the rooms he had visited, were familiar. He stayed one night in each, despite having rented West's flat. He considered it to be his research. They had to meet the set criteria. He would require the keys so he had pocketed them. The names he had given, details of the work he was doing in Harrogate and the addresses he had registered were all part of the mechanics of the game, the game that he had created.

Opening the bedroom door to find Alan flaked across the made bed was a rewarding sight. The red glow from the headlamp he wore gave enough light until he parted the curtains slightly. The blaze of the orange from the streetlights brought with it warmth. From the bag he removed the sheath. It would all be over in minutes.

***

April made herself a third coffee. Sleep seemed impossible as she watched Ralph's legs twitch. He was probably running after some ball in a distant and deep dream. She found it difficult to remove Drakes's face from her thoughts as she ran the consequences of the story over in her head. *What ifs* seemed a huge part of that rewind process as different scenarios tumbled in her mind's eye. What if Felicity not only had an affair with Drakes but also with Carruthers? What if Felicity's mother told Colin what she had witnessed, even mocked him? What if Colin had manipulated the incident with the stepladder, positioned it after striking or pushing her against the object that killed her? She really needed more information. What if Boardman knew of her initial infidelity, suspected Carruthers, discovered in fact that they were having an affair. That would suggest the swift exit of them both. She could almost hear Cyril's words now. *What ifs count for nothing without hard facts. You and I both know that.* He would be right. She looked at the kitchen clock. It was 3.15.

"Walk, Ralph." She summoned as much enthusiasm into her voice as she could muster.

The dream over, Ralph yawned and looked up.

"The Stray awaits, big man. Come on and then I need to feed you and get into work. Facts need finding, they'll never find themselves."

***

It never ceased to surprise him how soft the flesh was as he ran a finger along Alan's unshaved throat. In this relaxed position the skin felt new. Alan's head twitched slightly, responding to the touch. Quickly, the plastic bag was pulled gently over his head and an electrical tie was drawn tightly around it. He moved away, sat by the desk and watched and waited. Alan's body started to twitch and his hands moved towards his face. The drug had really taken hold and they flailed, displaying little control.

Guttural noises seemed to be adequately trapped within the bag as the arms slowly came to rest across the white sheets. It would not be long now. There were a few spasms and Alan's legs twitched, this time more forcibly but the bag seemed to have formed a death mask drawn tightly against his facial features.

Once he could no longer detect movement, he removed the bag. The neck, now exposed again, allowed the edge of the glass to run smoothly, slicing the flesh with such ease, causing droplets of warm blood to bead, ooze and run. Over and over again he passed the glass edge over the skin's surface, each time using a different level of force. The start point was always from the same side until it was time for the final cut using the last of the glass shards. On this occasion it dug deeply, severing and slicing all in its path. The wound curled slightly at the edges, like a flower's petals opening to reveal the richness of colour within.

After returning the glass back into the sheath, he removed a small bottle. He needed the tweezers to extract the small, used razor blade head to secrete it behind the washbowl pedestal. It was evidently not a place cleaned very often considering the degree of dust, fluff and other detritus in the room. A discarded cotton earbud looked particularly disgusting. He then found Alan's phone and dropped it into his bag.

Listening at the door for any sounds of movement, he took another swift survey of the room as he prepared to leave. Closing each door in turn he ensured that they were all locked. Within minutes he was in his car.

Chapter Thirty

April had brought the coroner's report on the death of Felicity's mother up on screen. As Quinn had accurately pointed out, there were unresolved questions and it was now clear why the said verdict had been given. She read through the interview with Drakes. Although it was fresh in her mind, she sought confirmation.

Checking the noticeboards, she observed that the findings from the *scribblers*, the name given to the forensic handwriting investigators, had confirmed that the lettering on Carruthers's right hand spelled the word, RITE. Inspecting the close-up images it was obvious to see that the loop on the letter R and the cross on the E could be misinterpreted for a D and a K. "Didn't know his left from his right. Only four fingers and he could see what it meant immediately."

Dan entered the incident room. "Heard you couldn't sleep. It's all getting as clear as the fog on a September day. This might help you to penetrate it. The DNA results on Drakes. I think you've found your man. Positive on the low copy number traces discovered on the dead men's clothing, the toenail clipping and on the mucus found in both rooms where the victims were located. Seems like a game, set and DNA match to me." A broad grin spread across his face.

April read the report and everything inside her screamed contradiction. Drakes did not have the intellect nor the stealth. She immediately thought about the man who had broken down and wept. She believed that she knew genuine emotional turmoil when she saw it and she was convinced that this was what she had witnessed. There was also an affinity, a strong bond between Tommy Boardman and Drakes. She scrutinised the test results. Something just did not gel.

***

Detective Chief Inspector Cyril Bennett carried the cup and saucer into his room. Unscrewing one of the batteries dangling from the charger plugged into the electric wall socket, he replaced the one in his electronic cigarette. The menthol vapour and the immediate shot of nicotine were just what he needed. He looked at his watch, shook his wrist and checked again. He was early by nearly an hour.

"Morning, I think, sir. Couldn't sleep so I came in to check a few things out. Poor Ralph didn't know what had hit him!"

Cyril laughed. "He's not the only one. Let me get this right. We may now have an historical rape to investigate against this Laird as he's known, whatever his name is."

"Lord Craimer."

Cyril looked up, gratified to receive the information. "A separate murder regarding the death of Boardman's mother-in-law and we're still working on the two murders here in Harrogate."

April slipped the DNA results document onto Cyril's desk. "When Drakes was in yesterday I gave him a drink and then took the liberty of sending for a RapidHIT test. Lo and behold this came back."

"What's the reliability of such a fast check?"

"Enough to arrest and hold him and to investigate further. What we need to do is to see if Gary Drakes checked into the B&Bs previous to the dates of the murders and take further DNA tests. We know that he's not on file for anything previous. We have him on record as registering and licensing firearms but he neither keeps arms nor ammunition at his present address. The tools he uses in the course of his work are stored there. I'd also like to talk to Felicity Brooke again in the light of Drakes's confession. There's more to this than meets the eye."

"Briefing is in sixty minutes and Brian is here in ten. Let's just make sure we have all the facts before the meeting. To use a sporting analogy, let's not go off half-cocked."

***

"Right. Good morning. You should be familiar with the latest developments. It looks to me as though we may well be closing in on our killer. We have the other developments but at this stage the historical rape can go on the back burner. The other death could be linked, so April and Quinn will be paying Felicity Brooke another visit after this briefing. I've already organised the arrest of Mr Gary Drakes for further questioning over the deaths of Kevin Carruthers and John Van de Meer. Owen will organise that. Drakes may well be responsible for the death of Felicity Brooke's mother too. He will need a solicitor present from the outset." He turned to an officer close by and made the request for him to organise it.

"Sir."

"The rest of you need to perform a final sweep of all of the evidence. Check and check again. Harry, once Drakes has been photographed, I want you personally to see if the owner of *The Grey House* and *The Victorian Guest House* recognise him as being a past client. Check their registers too. Also send it to facial recognition to see if he pops up anywhere else."

***

Jim West had also found sleep to be a stranger. He had to admit to being thrilled that the escape room had not only been a success for the client, but also a personal triumph for him. To have such a well-versed gamer pay him compliments was more than he could have hoped for. After the previous two volunteers had failed even to follow the most basic of instructions, he was now reassured that the level of the clues he had designed was appropriate. He was, however, angry that neither of the first players had responded to his offer to go through the clues with him in the hope that he could learn from them.

He wandered towards and then down Montpellier Hill, crossed by *The Crown Hotel* before wandering along Royal Parade. Pausing briefly, he admired the tree-lined cobbled Crown Place, a pedestrian street that ran alongside the beautiful and historical Pump Room Museum. Even in the weak light of early morning it retained its splendour. How he loved this town.

Passing through the gates of Valley Gardens, he decided on the lower of the two pathways and within minutes he was surrounded by the park's natural beauty. He stood momentarily and let the light breeze blow on his face. He thought of Valerie. She had been so concerned for him. Checking his watch, he decided that he would call her within the hour, he owed her that at least. Turning to leave he took the route towards the upper path. The public noticeboard came into view and it was one particular poster that drew his attention.

***

Cyril had briefly returned to his office when he received a call. It was 8.40.

"Where? The normal procedure. No one in or out, including the guests. Forensics?"

"Owen!" His voice carried through that area of the building.

Owen popped his head round the door.

"We've got another bloody body, another guest house and another with lacerations to the throat. Where the bloody hell was Drakes last night and what time did he leave here?"

Chapter Thirty-One

The road was closed off by the two, thin plastic tapes that ran from the railings of *Grants* guest house, over the pavement and to the opposite side of the road. Only two parked cars were trapped within. Twenty minutes earlier the restricted area had been broader but had now been checked for evidence. Cyril and Owen had parked in the middle of the road behind the two CSI vehicles, both small vans. A police officer stood nearby. Even at this stage a few inquisitive neighbours had started to spectate and chat with each other.

"Déjà vu, Owen. Déjà bloody vu." They stood at the tape looking first at the step plates that made their way towards the front door. Small raised squares made from plastic were being collected and replaced by a roll of what appeared to be blue carpet. The Crime Scene Manager waved and moved towards them. "Will need you suited and booted I'm afraid gentlemen."

"We've been luckier with this one, sir," the CSM announced. "The victim had requested an early morning call and that means a knock on the door in this place. That was at 07.30. Breakfast commences at 08.00 on a Sunday so we've asked people to stay in their rooms until Forensics have checked the route from the door to room 4. The scene's protected and some hearty people are leaving using the fire escape. Owner's arranged for them to have their breakfast in the B&Bs close by. Once we've finished, their day can, let's say, be service resumed."

Once they had donned the protective gear, they made their way through the two doors and into the hallway. It was a typical Victorian terraced house. Doors led from the hall and the staircase ran immediately to the right-hand side. Cyril glanced at the door marked *Private*. It was ajar and Cyril could see a police liaison officer sitting with a couple. He knocked.

"DCI Bennett and this is DS Owen. May we?" The introduction was to all three people but the request was directed at the officer.

"Please. This is Anthony and Rosy. They run *Grants* and have done for the last seven years. Rosy found Alan Bowen this morning."

Cyril looked at Rosy. His expression could neither be construed as affable nor sympathetic; it was a mix. Rosy simply nodded, her hands trapped between her knees. Her husband sat with a protective arm around her shoulders. He was wearing a clean, white chef's jacket in preparation for the breakfast service.

"He was such a kind young man. Why would anyone do this?" She looked up, her eyes pleading for some understanding of what she had just witnessed. Shaking her head in disbelief, she continued. "And to kill him like that…"

"What time was this?"

The liaison officer moved towards the door. "She needs a minute or two, sir. She found him at about 07.45. She and her husband couldn't raise him and wondered at first if he'd returned home. Wouldn't be the first time a young man booked in and then had a better offer from elsewhere. She went to get Anthony and the master key. They have a procedure. Knock again, open the door slightly and call, *House Keeping* and then either go in or leave depending on the guest's response within the room."

Cyril fully understood hotel procedures but remained patient.

"There was no response so Anthony went in first leaving Rosy on the landing. He closed the door, locked it and called 999. Nobody has entered the room apart from…" she flicked her head towards Anthony "…and then only one or two steps."

"What happened then?"

Anthony spoke. "We were told to close off that area of the building along with the entrance and the route to the front of the hotel. We were asked to check if there had been any damage from a break in, windows or the fire exit but there was none. Guests wishing or needing to leave were requested to do so by an alternative exit. We managed to get breakfast organised with other guest houses just along the road. We're a tight group and help each other out as much as possible. After all this could have been any of them."

Cyril knew that only too well.

***

Jim West had managed to get a coffee but had now lost his appetite. His feelings were ambivalent. Where he had been filled with an excitement from the success of the previous night, he was now utterly confused. Nervously he kept checking his watch. He did not want to call Valerie too early but he was desperate to talk. There were two more people chatting in the corner and one reading a newspaper. He stared out at the traffic that seemed to constantly stream down Parliament Street. His nerves fluttered as an ambulance went by. There was no siren but the blue light from the pulsing strobe flashed across the café's walls. For the next five minutes he would move the spoon in the froth on top of the coffee.

***

The two police cars turned into the driveway of the site at Brompton-on-Swale. One continued towards Chalet number 4 and the other blocked the road by Reception. People were already in the building as it was also the site's general store. A couple walking a dog moved to one side and watched.

Three officers climbed from the car, two of whom were uniformed and moved towards the chalet. The detective waited a short way back. Within minutes the door opened. Drakes stared at them, an old dressing gown wrapped around his thin frame.

"Gary Drakes?"

Drakes nodded and looked at both officers in turn.

"Mr Drakes, we are arresting you for the murders of Kevin Carruthers and John Van de Meer. You do not have to say anything, but it may harm your defence if you do not mention, when questioned, something which you later rely on in court. Anything you do say may be given in evidence."

Drakes's mouth opened but no words were emitted. He simply brought his hands to his face.

"Maybe you should dress and then we can get you to the station."

Within five minutes the forensics team was on site and the tape barrier was in place.

***

As Cyril and Owen stood at the bottom of the stairs the police doctor appeared at the top. "Cyril, we must stop meeting in such familiar circumstances. Dr Pritchett tells me you're now the proud owner of a classic Bentley motor car. I have to admit that I'm a little envious. They were Britain's very best."

Cyril had neither the time nor the patience to listen to drivel and was annoyed that his personal business was known within the Harrogate medical circle. The expression on Cyril's face suggested that this particular conversation was indelicate but Owen defused the moment.

"You'll have to join the queue to have a ride in it, doctor. I think I'm first followed by about forty people back at the station. Probably be a wreck by the time you get your turn."

The doctor laughed and patted Owen on the sleeve. "Right, dead about six hours. Incised wounds... again plural you note, gentlemen. As with the previous two cases, the edges to the incisions are red and swollen and adherent with blood trace and lymph. However, in this instance the neck injuries were the only injuries. Had we not had the previous two deaths we might have considered suicide but as yet there is no sign of a blade... And gentlemen, although the cuts match those of the previous two victims, there is no post mortem damage as we found with the other two."

"No amputation?" Owen quizzed.

The doctor shook his head and continued. "Interestingly, the injuries are typical of glass cuts. Each time the blade, for want of a better word, has been drawn across the throat with ever-increasing force. Looking at the victim's eyes I will also not be ruling out asphyxiation as the primary cause of death..."

Cyril considered the term, *primary cause of death,* believing that you could only die once.

"... And so the throat incisions in this instance could prove to be posthumous. No removal of body parts this time, just injuries to mimic the previous murders. At this stage in the inquiry, Cyril, it's the same man for me."

Chapter Thirty-Two

Quinn had parked the car in the identical spot as on their previous visit and they were now facing Felicity Brooke. On this occasion she had neither the cup and saucer nor the cat on her lap. Her demeanour had changed after confessing that she had in fact conducted affairs with both Drakes and Carruthers. There was a supercilious air about her. She was neither embarrassed nor contrite.

"It's the anti-depressants he takes, erectile dysfunction is a side effect. If I were to be honest though he'd lost interest in me as a woman. I was convinced he was seeing someone else. Drakes wasn't the first either. Felt sorry for him, not many lights on upstairs. He was really upset afterwards too. It was all my fault. I might be getting on in years but I'm certainly not a nun. I had an itch and I needed it scratching and he was the closest real man. Worryingly, he wouldn't perform again though. That was bad for the ego but I understood his concerns when I even offered to pay him. He couldn't abuse my husband's hospitality but he didn't use those words, obviously. When Carruthers started renting the flat it made things so easy, a bit like the film, *The Graduate*. We were as regular as clockwork. When Colin went out and if Kevin was home..."

"Did your mother know about your affairs?"

Felicity laughed. "She never could stand Colin, thought he was insipid, feeble and on the make. I think the final nail for her was when he was medically discharged from the army. *Not a real man,* she would say to me. Not like your father."

"Did you know your mother saw you in the shed with Drakes, on that occasion?"

"Why do you think I chose the shed?"

Quinn found it difficult to comprehend the difference between the woman they had interviewed previously and the woman now facing him.

"Do you believe Drakes is capable of murder?" Quinn asked.

"Always killing, rabbits, pheasant, badgers. You name it, he could kill it, skin it and cook it."

"A human being, Ms Brooke. Could he kill another human being?"

"Drakes? Never. Now Colin, Christ he could kill. The rows we had. He would go off like a firework for the smallest thing. When we discussed Kevin I thought he was going to go into the flat and kill him. He came in with some tool from the shed threatening to bash his brains in and gouge his eyes out. However, what he said he would do and what he actually did were two separate things. He used to just go off to the pub slamming every door he could."

April looked at Quinn. "May DC Quinn take a look in your shed?"

Felicity held her hand out as if pointing the way.

***

"Valerie, sorry, yes I'm well aware of what time it is… yes and I'm aware that it's Sunday. Look, I really need to see you. I need your help and I need you to look at something. Right now, I'm up by the Cenotaph, in Caffè Nero on Cambridge Crescent. I'd be so grateful if you could come. I need you to walk with me to Valley Gardens."

"You've not found a hand have you, Jim?" There was anxiety in her voice and Jim could hear her fear in the question.

"No, please hurry."

***

211

Drakes sat in the interview room and an officer stood by the door. A buccal swab had been taken but Drakes had neither protested nor spoken since his arrival. He simply sat, a frightened man confused, not only by the previous evening's interview in this very room, but by the word *murder* swirling in his mind. It just kept going round and round. His hands shook involuntarily and he rocked ever so gently backwards and forwards.

**

Bennett watched as the CSI moved up and down the stairs while Owen checked through the Guest House register. His finger tapped a page. "Got you! Two months ago we have a Gary Drakes booked in. Room four, same as the poor sod upstairs." He turned to look at Cyril and grinned. "Drakes's chalet is also number four if I'm not mistaken."

The liaison officer popped her head round the door. "Sir, this might be important. Rosy just informed me that she never saw the man who booked the room. It was a telephone reservation but a letter was left addressed to Mr Bowen in Room Four. On arrival, Bowen asked her to book him into the Mykonos Restaurant for nine-thirty last night. He'd picked up the card from the lobby there, on the table."

Cyril approached the table and picked one up. "So the room was booked by someone else?"

The officer nodded as Cyril went back into the room and sat facing Anthony and Rosy. "You have a name in your register, a Gary Drakes. Two months ago. Does that name bring anyone to mind?"

Both looked at each other and shook their heads. "Nope, can't recall. Look we have so many they become a name in a book and not a face, unless, of course, they are regulars and we have many of those."

"And the letter he received?"

"It might still be in the room, I don't know. It was simply pushed through the letter box."

Cyril left to consult one of the CSI officers. Within minutes she had returned holding a plastic bag. It carried its internal CJA label. Although it was not the whole envelope it was clear that the discovery pleased Cyril. There was nothing more he could do there until further tests were carried out. He had been informed that Drakes had arrived at the station but he needed to call at Mykonos Restaurant first to see if Bowen had dined there.

***

Jim was sitting in the café window in one of the deep leather chairs and as soon as he saw Valerie he sprang up and went to the door. She could see immediately that he was troubled and his lip quivered. "Sit, I need a coffee and you can then talk to me as we're going nowhere until you calm down."

"They're the two people who tried the game. I know it. Why I didn't realise this before I don't know. To think they..." He said nothing further.

Valerie put her hand on his. "We need to report this." She could also see his partner, the one who rented the apartment above his shop. It was her Svengali gift. She could envisage him, she could detect three keys in a gloved hand, the bedroom, the long thin pink-coloured glass. She saw the sawing motion back and forth. She shivered.

Jim observed. "Are you alright, Valerie?"

"Someone just walked over my grave, Jim. I'm fine."

"I could contact the officer who came to talk about games, he was pleasant enough. I have his number in my phone." Jim removed his mobile and checked through the address book. "Here, Harry Nixon. Nice man." He tapped the number and heard it ring.

"Is that Harry Nixon? Jim West. Sorry to trouble you so early at the weekend but I've just seen a poster featuring the two people who were murdered. It was on a public notice board in Valley Gardens. This might sound strange but they both played my new escape game; they trialled it, they were volunteers. Strangely they said they'd review it but neither did, mind they didn't escape so I thought it was possibly sour grapes. Never believed it was because they were murdered." There was a pause. Valerie squeezed his leg desperate to hear all of the conversation. "By the Cenotaph, yes. Ten minutes. Okay."

"Well?"

"We're being picked up and taken to the police station. He wants me to look at some pictures and give a statement. Will you come too, please?"

"Of course, Jim."

***

Cyril checked his watch. It was approaching 9.45. The skeletal grey structure that supported the awning seemed bleak but the flower edged decked area added a certain warmth. The tables and chairs that would normally fill the area were stacked inside. A police car was already outside as Cyril had called ahead for him to get in touch with the owner who was waiting inside, sipping a coffee.

Cyril smiled and held out his hand. "DCI Bennett and this is DS Owen. Sorry to trouble you so early. No doubt a busy night last night."

"We try, sir, we try. How may I help you?'

Cyril explained and the owner brought out the diary. "9.30 you say? Yes, a Mr Alan. Rosy from *Grants* booked it for him. Funny, he called in earlier and left an envelope. Said if a friend comes... just a minute." He went into the back returning with a crumpled envelope. "A David Hale, we were to give him this. He didn't come and neither did Alan. No show. It happens, but we don't usually get an envelope. Sorry for the state it's in, it was in a waiter's pocket. Can I get you a coffee?"

Owen was about to accept but Cyril declined, thanked him and left with Owen and the officer in his wake. Cyril sat in the car and looked at both sides of the envelope. "Now why would he leave a letter in a restaurant that he was going to eat in later, Owen?"

"In case he was going to be a little late?"

"He'd booked for one, not two."

"In case he failed to eat there?"

Cyril raised his eyebrows, removed a small penknife from his pocket and sliced the narrow end of the envelope. He looked inside. Slipping on some gloves he squeezed it open and used two fingers to take hold of the contents before slowly extracting the letter. It was folded in two. Opening it he turned to look at Owen. "Look what we have here."

***

Quinn returned with a wooden tool, a t-sectioned handle with a metal conical pointed end. It was about thirty centimetres long. He held it in his gloved hand.

"That's it. I thought he was going stab him with it but he had other ideas."

***

Jim and Valerie were standing outside the café when the police car pulled up and an officer lowered the driver's window. "DC Nixon is at the station. Please."

Jim opened the rear door for Valerie and he climbed in the other side. Within ten minutes they were turning down Beckwith Head Road. Minutes later they were walking through the rear door of the police station.

***

Brian Smirthwaite looked at Drakes. "I really didn't expect to see you so soon, Mr Drakes. Why didn't you tell us all about Carruthers and Van de Meer. It would have saved us so much time."

"I told you the truth yesterday, all of it."

"*The Grey House, The Victorian Guest House, Grants B&B.* They would mean absolutely nothing to you?" Brian studied Drakes's response carefully. He shook his head.

"Nothing, no."

"When was the last time you saw Kevin Carruthers?"

"I told you, he asked me to meet him in Harrogate, at the games thing. I did. Also the guy with the foreign name, I met him too. He was Kevin's friend. I think they'd met before but... I've done nothing, only what I said yesterday."

***

"What the bloody hell is all that?" Owen did not mince his words. He just looked across at the squiggles on the headed notepaper.

"That, Owen, is something you don't often see now but you used to, in fact, at one time all good coppers could write that. It's shorthand."

"Looks like that Egyptian writing to me, hieroglyphics."

"Come on, we need to get this translated and I know just the person." Cyril removed his phone and within two minutes the call had ended.

"Hospital, Owen and quickly."

The car pulled up outside the hospital and Cyril climbed out. "Wait, I'll not be long."

Margaret Leach was waiting for him and gave him a welcome hug. "You're a sight for sore eyes, Cyril. Still detecting?"

Cyril grinned. "No better offers. Still running the show, Margaret?"

She hit him affectionately. "What's this you want turning into English?"

The sheet was now trapped in a sealed, transparent plastic bag but the content was still legible. She read it out loud. Cyril switched on his phone's voice memo.

If you're reading this then you need to go to the police. I received an invitation to the escape room from the guy we met in The Coach and Horses. I was uncomfortable with the set up from the word go but if I refused then I knew he'd ask you. I was booked into the B&B you see above and I have to meet him at the library at 7 tonight. Whatever happens this evening will happen but if you receive this go to the police and don't accept any invitations.

Alan.

"Not too bad shorthand, Cyril. Room for improvement though. Send him to me."

"That might be sooner than you think, Margaret, but he'll be paying a visit to Julie first."

She looked at Cyril and then the smile left her lips. "Oh. I see."

Chapter Thirty-Three

The incident room was humming even though officers were busy with investigations. The latest info board drew Cyril's attention. According to the registers at *The Grey House* and *The Victorian Guest House* a Mr G Drakes had booked in on one previous occasion. He had occupied the same room as the victims. There was also an addendum; he had left on one, and possibly on a second occasion without returning the keys.

Cyril chewed his nail as he reread it. "If I were planning a future murder, would I leave my real name? No! Is someone setting you up, Mr Drakes and if so, why?"

April and Quinn entered. "What a difference a day or two makes. We saw a real transformation, sir, even under caution. For a sweet lady to turn into a femme fatale so rapidly and to exhibit no shame, it was mind-boggling. She had affairs with Drakes and Carruthers and from what she remarked, Colin knew, as did her mother. Colin even threatened to kill Carruthers using a tool we found in the shed. The courier has taken it for immediate forensic testing."

"Was that the reason Carruthers was asked to leave? Obviously, her mother didn't see that as she was dead by that point."

"Ms Brookes kindly pointed out that Drakes was not her first. His story stacks up. He had sex with her only the once. You know, I really think that poor bastard Drakes is being set up and he doesn't have the nous to see it or understand what the hell is going on."

"So where is Colin Boardman now?"

***

Jim West was describing what he had witnessed and then referred to the escape room. "Remember that games night when I said I had a project about which I couldn't speak at the time?" Harry nodded. "Well that was it. A friend of mine, well, an acquaintance if the truth be known, and I went into partnership, nothing legal just a toe in the water. I had the shop under the flat doing nothing and so it seemed like a good idea at the time."

Valerie could not keep quiet any longer. "Mr Nixon, I have a gift I believe to be special. I can look at you and see you as a sad man. You are, in my head, going through the first stages of a divorce and you've let yourself go. You feel guilty." She stopped abruptly. "No, that's not you, it's a colleague but you know about it and are protecting him." She closed her eyes. "Funny name. Anyway, Colin, this chap Jim's with, who rents his shop's apartment, is a bad one. Knew from the moment I set eyes on him." She now had Harry's attention. Only he knew that Brian Smirthwaite was going through a rough time at home and that distracted him from what she said later.

"I saw them arrive last night and to me it was so disconcerting."

Harry raised a hand. "Who arrived and what was wrong?"

"The young man and the tramp." She turned to look at Jim. "Tell him."

"We had a young man trial our escape room last night. His name was Alan Bowen..."

Valerie realised from Harry's expression that the name had hit a nerve.

"Who's we, Jim?"

"Me, Stan and Colin Boardman."

"Say the last name again."

***

It took precisely five minutes for Cyril to arrive at the interview room where Harry, Jim and Valerie were seated. He was carrying photographs of Drakes, Tommy Boardman and Colin Boardman. He also had a recent photograph of Alan Bowen found on a social media site. They were introduced.

"Please look at these photographs and tell me if you recognise any of these men." He showed a picture of Drakes first. Jim shook his head. Valerie looked too. She lifted up the photograph and observed every detail. She turned to Harry and placed it face down on the table, her hand resting upon it.

"He's a simple man, honest and trustworthy but one who has a good deal of hurt in his life."

Harry just looked at Cyril before handing Jim the next photograph of Tommy Boardman. His response was the same as with Drakes's photograph. He then passed it to Valerie.

"He has a look of your Colin Boardman but this man is not the same. He's contented, loyal and honest. A countryman."

"Have you ever seen him before, Valerie?" Harry asked, fascinated by the woman's intuitive thought processes.

"Never, but I've seen either his cousin or his brother."

When Harry passed the photograph of Colin Boardman to them both the reaction from Valerie was instant. She moved back from the table and raised her hands as if in defence.

Jim studied the photograph and responded. "He rents my apartment, has done for some time."

The details of their relationship were discussed and recorded and throughout the conversation Harry watched the expression on Valerie's face. It was clear that from their one meeting she had seen a side to the man which made her take an immediate dislike to him. However, it was the fourth picture that brought the most reaction.

"That's Alan Bowen, the young man who escaped last night. Bright as a button." Jim smiled for the first time since entering the room.

"He's dead," Valerie said rather matter-of-factly, turning her eyes to Cyril and then to Harry. "Please, on this occasion tell me I'm wrong."

Nobody needed to confirm her suspicion; the silence and their expressions said it all.

"I saw him arrive at Jim's. He was wearing sunglasses and headphones. I thought they were drunk."

It took some time for Jim to explain. He was requested to leave his address.

***

Cyril brought the team together in the incident room. Drakes was happy to be left alone as were Valerie and Jim.

"Let's put Drakes to one side. Even though we have DNA evidence from the first two sites they could have come from Boardman's house in Richmond and been planted in the room. They were definite items and if, as we believe, this was planned some time in the past, that's not beyond the realms of possibility. If we find something connected to it in this new site we know it was more than likely planted. He was in here until late, then he would have had to organise himself, know where people were and then attack them. He neither has the intellect nor the ability to plan anything long term. He certainly wouldn't have registered in his own name in the places where he planned to commit murder."

"What about Jim West?" Harry asked.

"You know him better than everyone here. Why would he come here? No, and the lady he's with is both fascinating and frightening with her Svengali gift. Does she know what a Svengali is... she knows more than she thinks but she doesn't know that." Cyril smiled.

Chapter Thirty-Four

Forensics had done a sweep of three buildings, the potting shed at Richmond, Drakes's chalet and Jim West's flat. To add further expense to Cyril's budget, Colin Boardman's car was slowly being dismantled by a team of forensic specialists.

Three photographs were pinned on the display board in the incident room. The first image showed the plastic blade head from a razor, the wooden dibber and then the bag showing the leather sheath, a ushabti figure and a small, glass pot.

"The blade found behind the sink had been used by Drakes but I suggest it was planted. The dibber is interesting as blood and minute strands of white hair were found trapped between the metal conical spike and the timber. This has every possibility of being that of Priscilla Brooke, Felicity Brooke's mother. It was retrieved by Quinn from the potting shed. Lastly, this bag was found in Jim West's flat which is now rented by Colin Boardman. Forensics have found glass particles that match those retrieved from the three victims. The ushabti figure contained DNA from West, Bowen and two others but the jar is the best of all finds. How they do this I don't know, just like I don't understand Valerie Thew's gift, but I cannot deny I'm impressed. This jar at one time contained the mucus, the nail clipping and the razor."

There was silence in the room.

Owen was the first to speak. "Why glass and why did Bowen write the letter in shorthand?"

"If you recall when we visited West's shop he still had his framing equipment. The glass and the cutters were there. Jim had demonstrated to Boardman how to cut glass and had given him a scrap of glass to practise on. It was unusual as it was a cranberry glass. We tested the oil found on that which was removed from the victims and it's a hundred per cent match with the traces on the cutters in the studio. Now the shorthand was interesting. I spoke with David Hale, Alan's friend who was also a keen gamer. He seemed to think that Alan had suspected something wasn't right. So, by writing it that way David knew it must have been written by Alan and also, anyone else reading it wouldn't have a clue. Remember to these guys life's a game."

"A game of life and death if you ask me, sir," Quinn commented.

Epilogue

It took less than twelve hours for Cyril and April to extract a full confession from Colin Boardman. He not only confessed to the murders of Carruthers, Van de Meer and Alan Bowen but also to killing his mother-in-law after she had provoked him about his wife's affair with Drakes. He confessed how she had mentioned Drakes's dibber and her calling him a loser, a weak and useless man so he had used it to kill her. He had staged the stepladders and faked her conversation. The fact that she was still alive when she arrived at the hospital was inconvenient but all she said was... Cyril looked at his notes... "*I just wanted it all to be finished... it to be over and done with.* In the light of what we now know, that could well mean the relationship between Colin and Felicity."

"But why remove the hand and the ears and then display them?" Quinn queried.

"Because they lost and they did not succeed because of their incompetence. He wanted to humiliate them just as he had been humiliated. She had tormented him by waving the dibber at him just before he killed her."

The room went quiet as they digested the facts. It was April who broke the silence.

"Drakes seemed relieved, so much so he gave me a hug!" April laughed. "Somehow I knew the poor man was innocent but I just had to prove it."

"Will you be trying out West's escape room, Harry?" Brian laughed.

"Not on your nelly. I've had enough games for one day. Besides I want to talk to you about something Valerie Thew said to me. Best over a pint."

"You fancy a pint, sir?" Owen asked Cyril, knowing full well he would not accept the invitation.

"Sorry, meeting someone." He winked at Owen.

***

Drakes leaned on the wooden rail and looked out across the shallow river. A fish broke the surface in the only pool close to the edge that was overhung by the roots of an oak. He tumbled the small figure in his hands. "Maybe you should have kept hold of this, Kevin, and had the luck yourself but I'm glad it's here with me. Thank you and…"

His words fell away, lost on the slight breeze and muffled by the weep of the water.

***

The Bentley pulled up as Julie came out from work. She had expected Cyril but she thought he would be on foot. She looked at the car and then through the windscreen at Cyril, who was grinning like a Cheshire cat.

"It's a surprise."

***

Jim dropped Valerie at the charity shop. "Thank you so much. I really can't understand how I allowed all this to cloud my judgement."

She leaned forward and kissed him. "You're a good man, Jim West. Remember that. I'll see you tonight. It's my treat."

Pushing open the shop door she was greeted by the familiar ring of the bell and the usual aroma. She smiled at Marjorie. "Been busy?"

Marjorie smiled. "You need a cup of tea. I can see it from your face"

***

Felicity Brooke nibbled a biscuit, the sleeping cat on her lap oblivious to the cascade of crumbs that fell onto its fur. *The*

Northern Echo, open on the coffee table, announced the arrest of Colin Boardman for the three murders in Harrogate.

A smile hovered on her lips and her free hand swept the back of the cat, its warmth both comforting and secure. How easy it all seemed now. "Men! You're your mother's daughter, Fliss. As mummy always used to say when I was a little girl... boys are so easy to manipulate if you get under their skin. You see, Tinker, getting inside their heads you leave no marks, no trace... nothing for people to interpret. What shall we do with dear Drakes do you think? Simply leave him be, yes?" she mumbled as the cat jumped from her knee. It stretched before walking towards the door. "Simple emotional manipulation, just like you do to me, Tinker. You want to go out I can see and your wish..."

The cat slipped through the door and she was left alone with her thoughts before folding the paper and dropping it into the wastebasket. "Tomorrow's kindling."

***

Heading north out of Harrogate, Julie slid along the bench seat and rested her hand on Cyril's knee. Neither spoke as the sun dappled the road before them. At Ripley they turned off the Ripon Road. In no time Cyril manoeuvred the Bentley into a car park and collected a bag from the boot.

"Fountains Abbey?" Julie asked, confusion and a faint disquiet written on her face.

Cyril smiled. "You'll have to trust me, doctor."

They soon reached the ruins of the Cistercian Monastery. He walked over to the bridge spanning the small river, the Skell, before putting down the bag. Removing a blanket he threw it over the bridge's low wall.

"I take it the seat will be okay and the view to your liking?"

"Cyril, you know I think it's the most beautiful place in Yorkshire but then... so is Brimham Rocks and Ramsgill and…" She laughed. "Only kidding. This is my favourite, honest."

He moved towards the bag, removed two flutes and a box, lifted the lid and presented it. "Would this be to the lady's taste?"

She read the word Krug and a date. "Have you solved the murders Cyril Bennett?"

He removed the cork, the popping noise loud and sharp, making her smile. He poured the two glasses.

"You have, haven't you, clever man?"

He stopped her from taking a sip. "Just a minute."

Putting his hand in his pocket, his fingers felt for the small box. He took it out and knelt before her… "Dr Julie Pritchett…" He opened the lid of the small blue box revealing his mother's engagement ring… "Will you… please… marry me?"

Julie put her hands to her lips, looked at the ring and then at Cyril, as a tear swelled in her eye.

Featured Artist

In this novel, Cyril takes delivery of a new piece of art, a bronze, bought at auction and titled, 'The Solitary Man' by the Irish sculptor, John Coen. In all my books I like to write a little about one of the pieces of artwork mentioned. In each case, I either own or have owned the specific work.

John Coen

1941-

John Coen's work comprises predominantly single edition small bronzes that are often quite surreal. Created as individual human forms or within groups of figures, the works have the appearance of stage sets, they are truly theatrical and therefore in keeping with the theme of 'Treble Clef'.

Coen's work bears similarities to the early work of Giacometti, and I feel there is a primitive rawness to the figures created. Many pieces appear to take on a nautical theme with specific pieces entitled, 'The Journey', 'The Missing Oar' and 'Longboat Oarsman'. One particular favourite of mine, and no doubt of Cyril Bennett's, is 'Ship of Saint Brendan the Navigator'.

Acknowledgements

Book eight in the Harrogate Crime Series and another change in direction. After completing the seven-book contract with my publisher it was time to become independent with this series; a decision not taken lightly. However, there were many positive reasons to throw myself into the deep end and swim alone.

Receiving the rights to the Bennett books has given me the impetus to learn new skills needed to publish in both Kindle and paperback format. It has given me the opportunity to look again at the books, to re-edit and where necessary revise the chapters. It is amazing what you learn when producing books over a period and I have been able to put all of that knowledge and experience back into the books.

After writing the first two books I realised that it would be a good idea to tag an artist featured within the book and this has been something I have done.

Designing new covers was also something I wanted to do. By pure chance I found what were for me, the perfect images. My sincere thanks to Kev Graham of Photolincs for those. Thanks to Craig Benyon at Create Print, Wigan, who patiently developed my design idea for the covers and made sure the end result was perfect.

As always, my wife, Debbie has stood by my side through the difficult weeks, getting to grips with formatting and printing, editing and reviewing and I shall never be able to thank her enough.

A huge thank you to Helen Gray who has worked hard to cast a professional eye over the text.

I feel now is the time to mention people who are the vital cogs in the success of many of my books. The book bloggers who give of their time to read and review the books. I will never be able to thank you enough.

Caroline Vincent, Bits about Books, has supported my work from conception and has been my guardian angel throughout. During the highs and the lows, she has always been there to encourage, cajole and be a critical friend. My sincere thanks, Caroline.

There are many unsung heroes who support the writing of a book, the ARC readers who give accurate feedback about the story and any inconsistencies. Stef O'Leary, Kath Middleton and Carrie Heap. Thank you.

Georgie and staff at Cordings, Harrogate who immediately offered to launch the book at the shop. I am honoured. Thank you.

Georgia from Imagined Things Bookshop, Harrogate has supported the series from the off. I was so proud to be labelled the shop's number one bestseller in 2018.

One of the most difficult tasks for me as a writer is to find character names. I welcome volunteers who would like to be featured within the pages of my books. On this occasion a thank you to Wendy Momen and Bill Clark for allowing me to add their names. To Emma and Martin Truelove also… surprise! I hope you like your characters.

I would like to say a special thanks to Bloodhound Books who originally saw something in my style of writing. We worked together for seven books and I shall always be grateful for their support for my work. I wish them well in the coming years.

As always, my thoughts are with Emily Shutt – a princess, a warrior and a little angel.

Andrew Forsyth – my sincere thanks for your fabulous support.

Stephen Barr – thank you for your support investigating the games world.

Escape room staff in Manchester, Harrogate and Warrington. My thanks for your help.

Dan O'Brien – thank you for your technical support.

Ian Cleverdon, thank you.

Fellow authors – Robin Roughley and David Evans – thank you.

The most important part of this section of the book is to say a massive **thank you** to you, the reader. Goodness, you have probably followed DCI Cyril Bennett and DS David Owen through thick and thin. I hope, like me, that you have come to know them and look forward to seeing what life has to offer between the pages of the next book.

If I have forgotten to mention anyone then please accept my sincere apologies.

Until book nine.

Malcolm

Printed in Great Britain
by Amazon